Addi looked at Jude over the rim of her teacup and slowly, conscious of her shaking hand, lowered the cup to the desk, trying not to spill tea on his brand-new expensive-looking carpet.

No, he couldn't possibly have said that, could he?

"I'm sorry, I thought you said that we should get married."

With his ankle on his opposite knee, leaning back in his chair, he looked relaxed, but Addi could tell he wasn't, not really. His green eyes were wary, and a muscle jumped in his rigid jaw. His shoulders were tight with tension, and he played with the laces of his dress shoes.

Addi tried to think of a response, and eventually settled on, "Why would you think that us marrying would be a good idea? It's the twenty-first century, Jude—people don't get married because of babies anymore."

Cape Town Tycoons

How do you resist an irresistible billionaire?

Lex and Addi had only ever had each other to rely on...until their absentee mother dropped two young sisters they never knew about on their doorstep. Now, everything Lex and Addi do is for them. They don't have time for love or passion—or to think about either!

Then Cole Thorpe and Jude Fisher come into their lives... The two tycoons are devastatingly handsome and infuriatingly tempting. So much so that working with them forces Lex and Addi to realize they aren't impervious to the attraction that Cole and Jude make them feel!

Read Cole and Lex's story in
The Nights She Spent with the CEO

And discover Jude and Addi's story
The Baby Behind Their Marriage Merger

Both available now!

Joss Wood

THE BABY BEHIND THEIR MARRIAGE MERGER

HARLEQUIN®
PRESENTS™

Recycling programs for this product may not exist in your area.

ISBN-13: 978-1-335-58442-7

The Baby Behind Their Marriage Merger

Copyright © 2023 by Joss Wood

Harlequin Enterprises ULC
22 Adelaide St. West, 41st Floor
Toronto, Ontario M5H 4E3, Canada
www.Harlequin.com

Printed in U.S.A.

Joss Wood loves books and traveling—especially to the wild places of southern Africa and, well, anywhere. She's a wife, a mom to two teenagers and a slave to two cats. After a career in local economic development, she now writes full-time. Joss is a member of Romance Writers of America and Romance Writers of South Africa.

Books by Joss Wood

Harlequin Presents

The Rules of Their Red-Hot Reunion

Cape Town Tycoons

The Nights She Spent with the CEO

Scandals of the Le Roux Wedding

The Billionaire's One-Night Baby
The Powerful Boss She Craves
The Twin Secret She Must Reveal

Harlequin Desire

The Secret Heir Returns
Crossing Two Little Lines
Just a Little Jilted
Their Temporary Arrangement

Visit the Author Profile page
at Harlequin.com for more titles.

CHAPTER ONE

STANDING ON THE balcony that ran the length of the Vane's ballroom, Addi Fields smoothed her hand over the slinky material of her satin slip-dress, conscious of the cool breeze blowing across her bare back. The dress, a deep navy-blue, drifted over her lanky body and, with its halter neck, looked demure from the front. It was anything but modest from the back, dropping exceptionally low to skim the top of her butt. Underwear had required a lot of thought.

Addi took a glass of champagne from a waiter and thought about the award she'd been handed earlier in the evening. One of the properties within the portfolio she managed for the hotel division of Thorpe Industries had won the award for small lodge of the year and she was comprehensively delighted. As there were rumours that Thorpe Industries was up for sale, she wasn't sure how long she'd get to enjoy the kudos that came along with the recognition.

Addi looked through the French doors into the busy ballroom. The room was packed with the hospitality sector's bigwigs: men and women who owned the most spectacular hotels, lodges and leisure operations on the continent. She was only there because Thorpe Industries was in a state of flux—Cole Thorpe had recently been gifted the company by his brother—and the hospitality division wasn't on his list of priorities. She'd asked for permission to represent Thorpe Industries, realising it was a great chance to network. Someone here might give her a job if she lost hers when Cole Thorpe sold up.

Her new boss was due in the country within the next few weeks, and Lex, her half-sister and best friend, would be driving him around Cape Town in her role as Thorpe Industries' part-time chauffeur. Maybe he'd let something slip; maybe Lex would overhear his plans, something that would give her an edge.

Addi could only hope.

Besides, she hadn't been prepared to pass up the opportunity to stay two nights in one of the best hotels in the country and eat five-star meals. It was a pity she didn't have the time, or money, to visit the hotel's award-winning spa.

Normally, her days consisted of leaving early to avoid the hellish Cape Town traffic, working ten hours straight and driving home, to be greeted by her energetic, noisy half-sisters. After the younger girls went to bed, she and Lex enjoyed a glass of wine and curled up on either end of their old sofa.

Most evenings they discussed their finances, with Lex telling her the girls needed money for a school trip, or new school shoes, or that a toilet was leaking, or that the gutters needed cleaning. She earned a good salary but, with three half-sisters to support, money never went far. It never had. And she'd never had the luxury of taking her salary and spending it on herself. She'd started working part-time at the age of fourteen, and initially most of her wages had been given to Joelle, her oh-so-irresponsible mother. Later, any money she'd earned had been given to Aunt Kate to help with the costs of housing and feeding Lex and her.

Addi rested the award on the balcony and lifted her face to look at the sky. She wondered when she could leave, at what point her escape wouldn't raise eyebrows—assuming, of course, that anyone would notice. She was a seriously small minnow in a tank full of sharks. She felt out of place and uncomfortable, but the chance to network and be seen by potential employers was worth any discomfort.

But in her slinky, barely there dress, she felt exposed and just a little naked. She far preferred her men's style white shirts, pencil skirts that hit her knee and her sensible pumps. Her ultra-short bright blonde hair looked trendy, but she kept it short because it saved time in the morning and, being naturally blonde, only required a touch-up every four or five months. She didn't have the time or money to spend on her appearance.

While she knew she should work the room, Addi simply didn't have the energy. She'd had a long day, culminating in attending a talk by Jude Fisher, owner and CEO of Fisher International. In his personal capacity, he owned several off-the-grid hotels and lodges. He and his grandfather before him—Bartholomew Fisher— were legends in the industry, owning some of the oldest and finest establishments in Africa. His hotel in the Seychelles was rated one of the best in the world, and their safari operation adjacent to the Etosha Game Reserve in Namibia had a waiting list of four years. *Four years.*

Addi had sat in the back of the room, her notepad on her lap, and listened to him expound on how hotels could become greener and more eco-friendly. Like her, he had a passion for sustainability, and his talk that afternoon had been well attended. She hadn't written anything down for the first ten minutes or hadn't taken anything in… She'd simply stared at him, drinking him in.

She wasn't normally so easily distracted but, thanks to Fisher's charisma, masculinity and the way he'd taken command of the room, she'd completely missed his opening greeting and introduction. Unlike the majority of the speakers at the conference, he'd elected to forgo a designer suit and had been dressed in navy chinos, a soft leather belt and an open-collared button-down white shirt, the sleeves rolled up to show muscled forearms.

Under the casual clothes was a body designed to make angels weep. He was tall, six-foot-three or so, and broad with it, his shoulders wide. Addi had been able to see the outline of a bold tattoo on his right pec through the cotton shirt and another tattoo on his left bicep. His hands and forearms showed the raised veins of someone who took his fitness seriously.

He also had a ridiculously sexy face topped with curly hair, styled off his face, keeping the sides and back short. Black stubble dotted his cheeks and jaw, hiding what she thought was a sensual mouth. His nose was long and a little off-centre, as if he'd broken it once and hadn't bothered to have it reset.

But it was his eyes that had caught and held her attention. They were a deep, dark green, the colour of ancient forests, framed by spiky lashes. His voice was deep and rich, hot chocolate on a cold winter's day. He'd worn leather bracelets and a trendy watch on his wrist, and he'd been utterly at ease in front of his audience.

When Addi had pulled her attention off his body and face and started paying attention to his words, she'd quickly realised he knew his stuff. She'd expected him to know the sector inside out, as the CEO of one of the most famous leisure groups in the world, but she hadn't expected him to do a deep-dive into the intricacies of sustainability and eco-friendly options for the leisure industry. Neither had she expected him to be so passionate about the impact their industry had on the environment. He'd spoken with assurance and knowledge, occasionally interjecting his speech with flashes of humour. He'd had all of the women and a good portion of the men eating out of his hand by the end of the ninety-minute presentation.

Thank goodness it had been recorded because Addi knew she hadn't taken in as much as she should've… Or anything much at all. He'd had some brilliant low-cost and effective ideas, but she couldn't remember one of them.

'It's a lovely night.'

She turned and watched as he lifted his shoulder off the wall and stepped out of the shadows. Her heart banged against her chest and she tightened her grip on her glass, the moisture in her mouth disappearing.

Talk of the devil and there he was…

Good grief, he smelled fantastic. She didn't recognise his cologne, but it made her think of a fresh maritime breeze or swimming in a blue-green, cliff-lined bay—fresh and fantastic.

Stop staring at him and think, Fields. You are in the company of one of the most influential men in the industry and, since there's a chance you'll be out of a job soon, this is an opportunity to make a good impression, to network.

But talking shop was the last thing on her mind. And it didn't look like one of the country's—the continent's!—most eligible bachelors was interested in networking either.

In fact, he was looking at her with interest in his eyes.

A *lot* of interest…

Ugh. What was happening here? She was cool and prickly, tall and lanky, and she wasn't the type to attract the interest of David Gandy loo-kalikes at social events. In fairness, she didn't go to balls or parties, clubs or bars, so she had no idea whether she was anyone's type any more. That was what had happened when at the age of twenty-six, and after a lifetime of disappointments, she'd undergone a monumental life shift. Not only had she been handed two half-sisters to co-raise and financially support, but her fiancé's promises to love her through good times and bad, to stick by her side through thick and thin, had evaporated as quickly as water on a hot stove.

'I'm Jude Fisher.'

Yes, she knew who he was.

'You were at my presentation this afternoon,' Jude said, coming to stand next to her on the balcony.

He'd noticed her—really? She'd sat in the second-to-back row behind a large man and a woman with big hair. Addi swallowed and nodded. 'I was,' she replied, cursing her croaky voice. 'It was interesting.'

He winced, humour flashing in his eyes. '"Interesting" good, or "interesting" boring?'

She raised one eyebrow at his comment. 'I wouldn't have taken you as someone who indulges in false modesty, Mr Fisher.'

He grinned at her sharp comment. 'I guess that'll teach me to go looking for compliments.'

'The room was packed, the attendees hung off your every word and you were mobbed afterwards,' Addi pointed out, trying to keep her smile from blooming.

'I noticed you slipped out as soon as I was done talking,' Jude said.

'Unlike the others, I didn't need anything clarified or any concepts explained.' Green energy was a passion, but she wasn't brave enough to tell him that she'd introduced measures to improve energy efficiency, reduce waste and recycle at all the accommodation establishments under her control.

She wasn't brave at all.

Jude gestured to her dress. 'You look lovely,' he said.

He didn't need to add that she'd looked very different that afternoon. She'd been wearing her corporate Thorpe Industries uniform of a white shirt, black skirt, pale-green jacket and low heels. Her uniform wasn't sexy or stylish, but it was free, and saved her from having to spend any money on work clothes. For that she was grateful.

'Thank you,' Addi said, catching the heat in his eyes. She'd been out of the man-woman 'I think you're hot' game for so long and she couldn't tell if he was interested or whether her imagination was running away with her. She gestured to his suit and lifted her eyebrows. 'That's a nice suit. Designer?'

Jude spread his arms and shrugged. 'I have no damn idea,' he admitted. He narrowed his eyes. 'Does it matter?'

'Not to me. Though it's a bold move, not wearing a bow-tie, or even a tie, when everyone else is wearing a tuxedo,' she commented, gesturing to his open-neck shirt under his black jacket.

'I forgot to pack a tie.' He shrugged, unconcerned. 'What are they going to do—toss me out?'

No, of course, they wouldn't. Frankly, the organisers would be grateful he'd chosen to attend the dinner and awards ceremony, because having him attend their conference had been a coup.

'Do you always do whatever you want to?' she asked, curious and not a little envious.

He lifted one shoulder in a careless shrug. 'Is there any point in doing anything else?'

Spoken like a man who'd never had to please anyone but himself. He had no idea what it felt like to be confined, to be forced into a situation over which you had no control.

'Don't you?'

'Don't I what?' she asked,

'Always do what you like, when you want to?'

She almost laughed but managed to swallow it, knowing that her chuckle would hold no mirth. No, she didn't. She worked, counted pennies, worked some more, drank wine with her sister and worked. Had she mentioned that? Before she could answer, he ran his thumb down her arm, his touch sending lightning bolting through her body.

She caught his hot gaze, saw desire flash within it and this time she had no doubt he was attracted to her. Heat flooded her system and goose bumps erupted on her skin. This was so strange, and she was miles out of her comfort zone. In some ways, she was standing outside of herself watching a movie, and she was in the starring role.

But tonight she didn't want to be normal Addi, the Addi who was super-responsible, who worked too hard and played too little. She wanted to be the woman who belonged in this dress, confident and cool, sophisticated and stylish.

Just for tonight, she wanted to be the type of woman Jude dated.

'As much as I can,' she finally answered. Her statement wasn't a lie. If she could have lived for herself, and been a little selfish, she would have. But at this point in her life she didn't have the bandwidth, emotionally or financially, to be self-centred.

Addi glanced down at his hand resting on the balcony, wondering how it would feel to have those big hands skim her body and explore her bare skin. She felt her nipples tighten and her heart rate picked up as heat bloomed between her legs. This was sexual attraction, hot and hard. It had been so long that she barely recognised it.

His eyes moved from her mouth and back up to her face. 'What is your name?' he demanded, his voice lower than it was before. It now reminded her of smoky whisky, of late nights and out-of-control sex.

'Addi,' she whispered.

'Addi.' He tested her name out on his tongue, his eyes not leaving her face. He touched her with nothing more than his thumb on the inside of her wrist and she felt as though she'd been plugged into an electricity substation. This was madness—the best type of madness, but still...

Madness.

Jude turned his head, and it was only when he stepped back that she realised how close she was to him, and wondered when one of them would make the move to close the gap between them. Jude took two glasses of champagne from the tray of a previously unnoticed waiter—honestly, an asteroid could strike in front of her but as long as Jude was within thirty feet she wouldn't notice!

He handed one to her, their fingers brushing. Addi lifted the glass to her lips and tipped it back, sighing when the dry champagne rolled over her tongue and down her parched throat. She turned to look out onto the gardens of the hotel, inhaling the combination of the smell of fynbos drifting down from Table Mountain and roses in the extraordinary rose garden below them. It was a sultry night, heavy with promise, the full moon peeking out from behind a thin cloud. It was the end of summer and, day by day, the sun would lose its heat and the night its sultriness.

She tipped her head up and looked at the night sky, wishing she could identify the individual constellations through the city haze. When she'd been a kid, star-gazing had made her feel connected to something bigger and better—what, she didn't know—and when she felt off-balance she still tipped her head up to the sky.

It didn't help much tonight; she was too conscious of the big, bold man standing next to her.

His arm brushed hers and he pointed up. 'You can just see the Southern Cross,' he told her.

Nope, the Southern Cross was to his right and down. She thought about keeping quiet, about letting him have his moment, but shook her head. She wasn't the type to play the dumb girl. 'You are about thirty degrees off,' she told him.

She expected him to pout—men never liked to be corrected—but he smiled, and she saw that famous double dimple appear on the left side of his mouth. His grin was wide and white, and his straight teeth flashed. 'Well, damn. I've been telling girls that's the Southern Cross for more than twenty years now.'

She smiled at him, enjoying his ability to laugh at himself. 'From now on, if I were you, I'd stay away from any star-knowledge seduction, Fisher.'

'Good to know,' he replied. He hesitated a beat before sighing. 'Damn, it was all I had. I'm never going to get a date again.'

She laughed and then rolled her eyes. 'Yeah, you're doomed,' she teased him. She did not doubt that the man had no problems picking up women.

That being said, while she didn't have the time to read the entertainment sections of online news outlets—she barely managed to keep up with the headlines—she'd never seen anything about Jude's personal life in the papers. There were no stories about him dating ballerinas, sportswomen, social-ites and celebrities. As a journalist had recently noted, he either had super-ninja skills at keeping his love life private or he was a monk.

Standing here with him, she knew he wasn't a monk.

'Do you often do this?' she asked. 'Approach strange woman on hotel balconies?'

'You're the first. I tend to keep my…' he hesi-tated '…romantic interests low-key. I think that what I do in my free time is my business and no one else's.'

Fair enough.

He leaned his forearms on the balcony and linked his hands together. When he spoke, his voice was more serious than she'd expected. 'And what has been written is exaggerated.'

She examined his face and saw that his mouth

was drawn into a thin line, and a muscle ticked in his jaw. 'Somehow the press always manages to get it wrong, or construct sand castles from a single grain of sand.'

He didn't like press reporters, that much was obvious.

'Why are you telling me this?' she asked, curious.

'I have no idea,' he replied. He lifted his champagne glass, tipped it up and drained the contents. 'When your eyes connect with mine, I feel like I need to tell the truth.'

'My eyes are just a very normal blue,' she informed him, a little confused. Sure, she was a blue-eyed blonde, but she wasn't anything special. In fact, she frequently wished she could have her sister Lex's exotic looks. She was a bold redhead with a freckle-covered face. People looked twice at Lex because she was interesting. Addi, on good days, was merely pretty. Unlike her fickle mother Joelle, she didn't have the Marylin Monroe sex-on-a-stick thing going on.

'Normal?' He scoffed. 'They are the colour of the sea at midnight, deep and dark and intensely mysterious.' He released a half-laugh and shoved his hand through his hair. 'Jeez, now I'm sounding like a greetings card.'

His words were smooth, but his delivery wasn't, and that was what kept Addi in place. She heard authenticity in his voice, seemingly caught off-guard by his attraction to her. She glanced down at the hand gripping the stem of his champagne glass and noticed the fine tremble in his fingers. Her eyes moved up and she noticed the tension in those broad shoulders, his bobbing Adam's apple and a hint of red on his cheekbones.

This man wanted *her*. The thought smacked her with all the force of a bullet train. And he was trying hard not to show it, was attempting to be the man about town the world thought him to be. She lifted her hand and touched his jaw with the tips of her fingers. The pads of her fingers skimmed his stubble, and she dragged her thumb across his bottom lip, her eyes locked on his.

She could see them, naked on a big bed, her skin pale in comparison to his tanned body. She could imagine the feel of the muscles of his back under her hands, his long legs tangled with hers, his dark head dipping to kiss her. She could feel the night air wafting in over their bodies from an open window and hear the sound of the party-goers in the ballroom below. They would be good together. He'd make her feel like a woman, strong and powerful. He'd make her scream, then sob, with pleasure.

She wasn't someone who jumped into a stranger's bed—one-night stands weren't her thing—but she knew she needed this night with

Jude. She needed to feel like a woman, to feel like herself, to be anything but the stressed-out worker bee, the responsible older sister, the one who spent her nights trying to stretch a budget that had no give.

She needed to feel, to be body to body, mouth to mouth, and enjoy an intimate, physical connection. She had one more night away from her sisters, one night to be someone other than the woman she normally was, and she knew she'd be regretful for ever if she didn't take this time, take this man...

Didn't allow him to take her.

Jude turned his mouth into her hand and kissed her palm, his tongue coming out to touch her skin. She tensed and closed her eyes, and the intensity of his touch reached her newly painted, pretty toes. If he could make her feel so much with one small kiss, what would happen if he kissed her properly, if she allowed him access to every part of her?

Jude held her head in his hand and his eyes held hers as he lowered his head, bending his knees a little so that he could touch her mouth with his lips. She'd expected hard and fast, but she got gentle and slow, a 'hello, I'd like to know more' kiss. She held his strong wrists as his lips explored hers, nibbling here, sliding there. She sighed and his tongue slipped into the small opening. Her tongue met his and two universes collided and merged.

Suddenly there was only the air he could give

her, his tongue feeding her hot, dark kisses. Pleasure spun her away, and she sighed when his hand came to rest on her bare lower back, his fingers flirting with the top of her butt. He pulled her into him, and her breasts pushed against his chest, her stomach resting against a fantastically long and hard erection.

Heat, desire, need and want ripped through her, as fast and unexpected as a hidden current in a sluggish river.

He groaned, palmed her breast and found her nipple with his thumb, eliciting another moan from her. He wrenched his mouth off hers and dropped hot kisses on her jaw and down her throat, sucking gently on the ball of her bare shoulder.

'I want you,' he muttered, his voice low and guttural. 'I wanted you when I saw you this afternoon. I want you now. Let me take you to bed.'

This was *her* time; this was *her* night. The night where she could be Addi, where she could be free. Free from responsibility, free to be herself. To feel, experience...

She stood on her tiptoes and dragged her mouth across Jude's. 'Yes, please.'

CHAPTER TWO

ADDI STARED AT the small window showing two blue lines and felt her heart go into freefall. Unable to believe what she was seeing, she picked up another test from the top of the toilet's cistern and peered down into that window. A flashing 'pregnant' pulsed in it. The third test also showed two blue lines.

There was no doubt that she was pregnant.

Addi sat down abruptly on the closed toilet seat and dropped her head between her legs, trying to get air into her suddenly too-small lungs. *Pregnant?* How? What? Well, the how she knew: she and Jude Fisher had made love twice—three times—eight weeks ago and somehow, despite her having been on the pill and he having worn a condom, one of his boys had met one of her girls.

She could explain the pill failing; she'd had a dose of antibiotics that week, and it was said that they could impair the efficacy of the contraceptive. But Jude had used condoms. They'd done everything right, everything they could to prevent a pregnancy, but here she was, a mummy-to-be.

How had that happened? And why had it happened to *her*?

Addi felt her stomach knot and her throat constrict. Standing up, she whirled around and flipped up the seat. She dropped to her knees in front of the toilet and heaved.

After rinsing out her mouth and splashing her face with water, Addi lifted her eyes to look at her reflection in the mirror. Two blue stripes ran under her eyes and her face looked blotchy, her lips chapped. Her eyes were bloodshot from spending too many hours looking at her computer screen and she'd lost weight, something she couldn't afford to do.

Addi gripped the sides of the basin and stared down at the plug, panic rolling over her in an insidious tide. She couldn't be pregnant, she didn't want to be pregnant—it wasn't in her five-or ten-year plan. It wasn't in her life plan at all.

And, God, how was she going to explain to Lex that she was pregnant via a one-night stand? They'd promised each other, promised themselves, they'd take precautions not to bring any unwanted children into their lives. They would *not* follow in their mother's five-kids-by-five-different-men footsteps. They'd be responsible, they'd be clever.

She'd failed on all counts.

And failure wasn't something she did, wasn't something she tolerated.

This was *so* Joelle, Addi thought, cursing herself—falling pregnant by a sexy guy who'd rocked her world, taking pleasure in a random encounter, was something her feckless mother would have done. Addi hated herself for giving in to temptation and sleeping with Fisher. Her mother was the sensual, impetuous one, prepared to put her pleasure over common sense, but Addi was not. She was the one who trailed behind her mother and picked up the messes she made. She was the one who'd rolled up her sleeves and gone to work, despite her broken heart, when Joelle had left two half-sisters for them to raise.

Addi stared at her shoes, fighting the tidal wave of anger threatening to consume her. Hadn't she been handed enough, forced to deal with more than most? She'd been born to the most irresponsible woman on the planet and she and her half-sister Lex had been lugged from house to house, room to room, depending on whom Joelle could seduce enough for them to take her two kids and her in. They'd missed meals and school, and their childhoods had been tumultuous. When Addi had been five or six, Joelle had married Tom and given birth to Storm, another half-sister. The years spent with Tom had been the happiest of her life, secure and stable.

Although she'd been so young, she understood that, easily bored, Joelle wasn't cut out for monogamy. When her mother told them they'd be moving on without Storm, who would stay with Tom, Addi had felt devastated but she hadn't been surprised.

Nothing good lasted for ever…sometimes it didn't even last three years.

The next years had been a blur, with too many faces and too many houses, and life had only made sense again when Joelle left them with her aunt Kate when Addi had been seventeen. The irascible old lady had given them their second dose of stability and, when she'd died, she'd left her house to Lex and her and a small insurance policy, enough for one of them to go to university. She and Lex had come up with a plan: Addi would go to university and get her degree in as short a time as possible. Lex would go out to work and her income, with the rooms they let to other female students, would pay for their living expenses. When Addi got a job, she would pay for Lex to attend uni.

She'd landed a fantastic job, Lex had enrolled

at university and Addi had started planning her wedding to the love of her life, the man she'd met during her first year at university. Dean had been educated, successful and ambitious, and when she'd moved out of their house and into his luxury Camps Bay flat, the plan had been that Lex would rent the additional room in the cottage to provide her with an income while she studied for her degree.

Addi had had everything under control, planned and perfect. The wedding reception was to have been smaller than Dean had liked, but Lex and Storm were to have been her bridesmaids and Tom, her ex-stepfather, was to give her away. Believing that nothing could go wrong, she'd even sent a Save The Date card to Joelle and asked her whether she thought she might attend the wedding.

Ten days after Addi had sent the email invitation, Joelle had flown back to Cape Town from Thailand, accompanied by two half-sisters she and Lex hadn't known they had. Joelle had asked Lex and her to look after them for the weekend and that was the last time any of Joelle's girls had seen their mother.

She'd gained two half-sisters and lost her fiancé. Despite Dean having tried to make it work—she had to give him that—Nixi and Snow weren't what he had signed up for and he hadn't wanted to share her, his home, or his life with two little girls. She'd asked him to postpone their wedding for a year, maybe two, to give them time to wrap their heads around her life changes—love couldn't fade that quickly, could it?—but he'd called it quits, blithely informing her he didn't love her enough...

That he probably didn't love her at all.

And, at that moment, Addi had finally grasped the lesson that life had been trying to teach her: that people would always let her down, normally at a time when she needed them the most. It was always, always, better to rely on oneself. And she would never put her faith in anyone other than her sisters again. She'd vowed that Joelle's girls would be smart, responsible, independent and *better* than their irresponsible mother.

But she, responsibility personified, was the one who was pregnant. Addi was embarrassed and furious, but she was also scared. After Dean had absconded, she'd imagined that, since she had no intention of marrying ever again, having children wasn't on the cards for her. And maybe that was a good thing because, unlike Lex, she'd never managed to fully connect with her half-sisters. While she'd gone to work and tried to keep their financial heads above water, Lex had scooped them up, dispensed hugs and kisses, dried their tears and listened to their rambling stories.

Okay, sure, she wasn't around them as much as Lex, but when she got home they didn't rush to hug her as they did Lex, didn't curl up into her lap as they did Lex. Hers wasn't the bed they ran to when they had bad dreams, hers wasn't the opinion or reassurance they sought.

Lex was warm and she wasn't. While she had Joelle's features, her blonde hair and blue eyes, she came across as being haughty rather than sensual. Being naturally shy and very guarded, she disappeared behind a cool mask and talked in a clipped, no-nonsense style, fast and sharp.

She knew her work colleagues considered her stuck up, and she was never invited to join the younger staff members for a drink after work or go to their houses for a barbeque at the weekend. They didn't understand that she had all the responsibilities her older colleagues did, children to raise, a salary to stretch.

And now she had a baby on the way. How was she going to work, have a baby, raise Nixi and Snow and support Lex so that she could finish her degree? And, with Thorpe Industries being put up for sale, she'd be out of a job in a few months. The thought of going through the stressful interview process, trying to impress and convince owners or managers that she was worth taking a chance on, pregnant or not, made her throat close.

Panic filled her. She needed to work; she couldn't be without an income. She had three and a half people relying on her—what was she going to do? What plan could be made? All she could do was send out her CV and look for a new job. But was that enough? She didn't think so.

As Addi stepped back into the stall to get her tests and bag, she heard the door to the bathroom open and a few seconds later she heard a familiar deep voice bouncing off the walls. 'Addi, are you in here?'

She could easily imagine Greg, her assistant, stepping into the ladies'. He didn't have a reticent bone in his body.

'I'll be out in a minute, Greg.' Jeez, couldn't a girl take half an hour to do three pregnancy tests and have a mini panic attack without someone hunting her down?

'Cole Thorpe is looking for you. He's tried to video-call you twice.'

Her head shot up and she swept the pregnancy tests into her bag. She walked over to the basin and flipped the tap to wash her hands.

'Did he say what the urgency is?' she asked Greg. Why did the big boss and owner want to talk to her? What was she missing? What hadn't she done?

'No, but he told me to find you and that he will be calling back in fifteen minutes.' He drew a circle in the air, gesturing to her gaunt face. 'You need to put on some lipstick and blusher, and I'll make you a cup of coffee.'

Her stomach rebelled at the thought. 'Make it a cup of rooibos tea and you're on.'

Greg stared at her. 'You hate rooibos tea,' he pointed out, frowning.

Yeah, but she'd hate throwing up in front of her boss more.

'So, it's settled, then? Addi will be your liaison between you and Thorpe Industries. Nobody understands the division better.'

Jude looked at the two squares on his screen, the smaller one containing the face of his friend Cole Thorpe, the larger one reflecting the very lovely face of his one-night stand from two months ago. Jude rubbed his hand over his jaw, dropping his eyes briefly to look at the small block showing his reflection. He looked reasonably impassive. Unlike Addi, he wasn't wearing a *what is happening here?* expression.

Cole's eyebrows pulled down into a frown and impatience flickered in his eyes. 'Guys? Has my sound cut out?'

Jude nodded and managed a thin smile. 'Sure, that's fine. Let me have a look at all your hospitality assets and I'll let you know what properties I am interested in.'

'I'll give you a better price if you take all of them,' Cole shot back. Jude sighed. He knew Cole wanted to rid himself of an inheritance he hadn't wanted or expected but, old friend or not, Jude wasn't going to buy hotels, lodges or camps that didn't suit his, or Fisher International's, needs.

But to make an offer, or even look at what his friend owned, he'd have to work with Addi. It made sense on a business level. Her title was Operations Manager, and she was, per Cole, the hospitality division's trouble-shooter. Judging by the wealth of documents he'd already received from Cole, she had spreadsheets to keep track of her spreadsheets, and every entity was broken down to the smallest cup, blanket and spare part. The woman was scarily efficient.

She also, Jude noticed, looked exhausted. With her hair slicked off her face and red lips, the woman on his screen looked cool and composed on the surface. But her eyes were dull with fatigue, and she'd lost weight since he'd last seen her. Yet his heart still kicked up and the fabric of his pants suddenly felt one size smaller. There was something about her that heated his blood, that made his heart stutter, that closed his throat.

And, whatever it was, he had to get over it before he met up with her again.

Talking of… 'I suppose we'd better check our diaries, Ms Fields.'

'Mr Thorpe has instructed me to make sure I'm available to you,' Addi replied in a cool voice. 'So I am completely at your disposal, Mr Fisher.'

His eyes met hers in cyberspace and he saw hers darken and flicker with want, or need. But an instant later they returned to being a murky blue. The woman on the balcony had fizzled and sparked; she had been sassy and confident, at ease in her skin. This Addi looked and sounded like a faded version of herself. In a very vague way, she reminded him of the way his mum had looked shortly before she'd died—worn down, exhausted, emotionally battered. He'd been young when she'd died from an ectopic pregnancy, just eight, but he'd had to grow up superfast, becoming self-reliant almost immediately. That was what happened when one parent died and the other checked out. Then checked out permanently by dying.

'I'll leave you to it,' Cole said, and with a tap on his keyboard disappeared from the screen. Jude made sure he was gone before resting his forearms on his desk.

'I didn't know you worked for Cole,' he said,

picking up a pen and tapping the end on his desk. He was working out of his study at his vineyard in Franschhoek, just an hour from the city. He glanced to his right, enjoying the view of vineyards rolling up to the edge of the saw-tooth ragged peaks of the Franschhoek Mountains. This was the first day he'd seen the sun for a long time, and when the next cold front rolled in they would be having weeks, possibly months, of cold and wild weather.

'How would you?' Addi asked, shrugging. 'We didn't spend that much time talking.'

He couldn't dispute her words. After that brief conversation on the balcony, he'd kissed her, she'd kissed him back and then they'd both been eager to find the nearest bed. His suite happened to be closest, and they'd spent the rest of the night, and half of the next morning, making love. He'd only left the room because he'd had a brunch meeting and when he returned two hours later she had gone.

He'd been disappointed but, when that faded, also grateful. Thanks to the call he'd received from Cole just before his presentation, enquiring if he would be interested in purchasing the hospitality division of Thorpe Industries Africa, he hadn't had the time for an affair, however brief. Cole's newly acquired company owned some amazing hotels, a few of which he'd be happy to add to Fisher International's portfolio. There were also a couple he wanted for his personal chain of eco-friendly accommodation. It would be a next-level deal and he had been working sixteen-hour days for the last two months.

That was what it had taken to persuade the Council of Three to agree to him even investigating the potential deal.

Addi turned at the sound of a knock on her door and asked him to excuse her for a minute. On his computer screen he watched her walking away. She had a spectacular butt and incredible legs, and he rubbed his hands up and down his face. He didn't need to be distracted by a woman—not now.

Acquiring the hotels and lodges for Fisher International would be tricky. It would be the first major acquisition he'd done since he'd taken over from his grandfather and, he estimated, would cost over two hundred million pounds. That sort of expenditure—*any* unexpected expenditure—needed his three-person board of trustees' approval.

Jude felt the familiar swell of frustration and annoyance. He owned Fisher International outright but, because his grandfather hadn't trusted his judgement, for ten years following inheriting the company Jude had to seek approval from three men his grandfather had appointed. He clenched his fist and leaned back in his chair, looking over the vines and out onto the mountains. Nine years had passed and he just had to deal with them for one more year. Then he'd have full control of Fisher International. He could take it public, sell it, even run it into the ground, and nobody could say or do a thing.

He. Could. Not. Wait.

Addi slid back into her seat and lifted her eyes to the camera. 'I'm sorry about that, I needed to take an urgent call from the hotel in Zanzibar.'

He had an idea of her role but asked her to clarify what she did for Thorpe Industries.

'I see myself as a back-up system for all the managers. I help with budgets and staffing issues. I source people and commodities. I authorise bulk-buying orders for all the hotels, like linen and toiletries. I don't do any direct marketing, but I keep an eye on marketing to make sure they are not going off-brand.'

It sounded like a lot for one person to do. No wonder she looked exhausted. Jude tapped his pen against the side of his desk. They needed to meet, as soon as possible. Partly because he needed to get a better, more personal handle on what he was looking at in terms of Cole's assets, and partly because he wanted to see her again.

She'd been on the edge of his mind for the last eight weeks, images of her—long legs, pale skin, him running his hands through her short hair, her elegant feet and the sexy moan she made when he'd slid inside her—ambushing him at entirely inappropriate moments. She'd burrowed under his skin, but he knew that working with her, the long hours spent poring over spreadsheets and figures, would cure him of any lingering sentiment. There was nothing that killed attraction quicker than spending long hours in front of a computer screen and arguing figures.

'When can we meet?' he demanded. 'This afternoon?'

'Where are your offices?'

'We are in the process of moving the company headquarters to a new building on the Waterfront, and while that happens I am working out of my home office in Franschhoek.'

Addi wrinkled her pretty nose. 'And when are you coming into the city again?' she asked, looking off-screen. He heard the tap of her fingers against her keyboard and assumed she was looking at her diary, trying to work out when she could fit him in.

Maybe she needed reminding that he was her first priority. 'I want to meet this afternoon,' he stated, his voice taking on an edge that suggested she not argue. He was being demanding but he needed to see her again, to look into those blue eyes, to inhale her sexy scent. Why? Why her?

Why hadn't he been able to get her off his mind?

Once he saw her again, he'd be able to move on, stop thinking about her and concentrate fully on his business and his career. That was what was important. His brief flings? Not so much.

'I'm free from two. I want an overview of the offerings, their unique selling points and their turnover and profit margins,' Jude stated.

Addi raised her eyebrows and, even though they were meeting in cyberspace, he felt the impact of her hard, blue-eyed stare. 'You're joking, right?'

When it came to business, he was always deadly serious. 'Do I look like I'm joking?'

'You want me to pull all that information together in, what…?' She glanced at the functional watch on her left arm, and Jude couldn't help thinking that something delicate and pretty would suit her better. 'In five hours? And that's including the hour travelling time to Franschhoek? Are you mad?'

'Are you telling me you can't?' Jude suspected that, while she might not be able to give him nuts and bolts figures, she had most of what he needed in that big brain of hers.

Her eyes narrowed and her mouth flattened. 'I could give you an overview by this afternoon—'

'Good. Give me your phone number and I will send you a GPS pin.'

Addi held up her hand. 'Will you let me finish, please?'

He leaned back in his chair, impressed that he didn't intimidate her. That could be because he'd been charming Jude when they'd met, or it could be because she'd seen him naked, but he suspected that Addi wasn't a pushover in general. He liked that. He far preferred people who pushed back than suck-ups and sycophants. He lifted his head in a gesture for her to continue.

'I can't meet you at two; I have a lawyer's appointment.'

Why was she meeting with a lawyer? Was there a lawsuit against one of the hotels he wasn't aware of? If he was going to be pulled into a legal fight, he'd pull out right now. 'What's the problem?' he demanded.

'It's a personal matter, Jude, nothing to do with Fisher International,' Addi said, and he heard exhaustion in her voice.

He caught the wariness in her eyes, and his curiosity peaked. 'Why do you need a lawyer?'

'Are you normally this nosy?'

No, he wasn't, not by a long shot. In reality, he frequently had to cut women off when they shared personal information. He wasn't interested in the minutiae of people's lives; he kept his interactions with the opposite sex as shallow as he could—movies, books, current events…bed. Women couldn't be trusted with his thoughts, feelings, memories or his heart. And, if they didn't know anything about him or his business, they couldn't pass anything on to the press. For the past ten years or so, that strategy had worked well for him, and he'd rarely made the news for anything other than his business successes.

When he didn't answer, Addi spoke again. 'I can be with you around four,' she told him. 'But I can only give you a couple of hours because I need to be back in town by seven.'

'Do you have a date?'

Where had that come from and why did he care? He cursed himself, wondering whether some idiot had hijacked his brain. She was now a work colleague, and he had no call to question her about her personal life. But the thought of her sitting across the table from another guy, laughing with him, talking to him—going to bed with him—set the lining of his stomach alight.

Addi looked down her nose at him and he had to admire her sangfroid. 'That has nothing to do with you, Jude,' she told him, her voice colder than an Arctic wind. She placed her elbow on the desk and massaged her forehead with the tips of her fingers, as if trying to rub away a headache. When she spoke again, her voice was low and a little haunted. 'I don't know if I can do this…'

Do what—meet with the lawyers? Work with him? Drive out to Franschhoek? *What?*

Before he could ask, Addi lifted her head, straightened her shoulders and inhaled deeply. 'Four o'clock today? Or would you like to suggest another time?' she asked, her fingers drumming the desk next to her keyboard.

He couldn't wait. He wanted to see her…see those spreadsheets, get working on acquiring those hotels, he quickly corrected himself. Acquiring Thorpe Industries' assets at a good price was an opportunity not to be missed, provided he could get the proposal past the trustees. He'd made two massive errors of misjudgement—both involving women he'd cared for—and they'd led to huge unintended consequences. And he was still paying the price.

Not even Addi could tempt him to wade in more than toe-deep. He was immune to any commitment that lasted beyond breakfast the next morning. He'd learned his lesson…

Women, people in general, couldn't be trusted.

CHAPTER THREE

THIS COULD NOT be happening to her, not on top of everything else! Addi gripped the steering wheel of her company car, her eyes blurring with tears, which wasn't a good thing when trying to navigate a busy highway. She blinked furiously and swallowed down a sob threatening to escape. She hit the button on the electric window and icy air instantly dried her wet eyes. She left the window open a crack, thinking that red-from-cold eyes had to be better than scarlet-from-panic-and-distress eyes.

Seeing her speed creeping up, she eased off the accelerator and glanced at the clock. She was going to be twenty minutes late for her appointment with Jude but that couldn't be helped. After leaving the lawyer's office, she'd stumbled to her car and sat there for forty-five minutes, trying to make sense of what she'd heard...

Addi felt another tide of panic rise up her throat and sucked in a series of harsh gulps.

She couldn't think about what she'd heard earlier; she could barely make sense of it. If she allowed herself to get caught up in that, she'd lose concentration and would find herself intimately connected with the back of a passenger bus or a heavy-duty truck.

No, she had to park it…just for a little while.

Her navigation system directed her to take the next exit and Addi moved across the motorway, weaving her car between a truck and an overloaded bus to scoot off. It had been ages since she'd been in Franschhoek, but she had too much on her mind to take in the pretty vineyards and the towering mountains. She was about to meet the father of the bean growing inside her, the baby she was still wrapping her head around.

Somehow, she needed to find the words to tell him she was pregnant, that the pill had failed and that one of the condoms he'd used had been faulty. How, in the twenty-first century, did that happen? Weren't they supposed to be foolproof these days?

There was little point in trying to figure out the *how*; she had to deal with what *was*. However it had happened, she was now carrying a mixture of his and her genes and she had no idea what she was going to do. Frankly, a baby was the last thing she needed in her life right now. Her job with Thorpe Industries was coming to an end, and there was no guarantee that the new owner, whether that was Jude or anyone else, would take her on. The law said that employers couldn't discriminate against employing pregnant women, but the law wasn't always applied in the real world.

She needed money to pay for the lawyers she'd undoubtedly need and to keep her family's heads above water. But, whenever she thought about making her baby problem go away, she couldn't finish the thought. She was embarrassed that she'd accidentally fallen pregnant and she couldn't afford a baby. She didn't have the time, finances or energy.

But she was keeping it. She couldn't *not*. And that meant telling Jude. And that was a conversation she really didn't want to have.

Turning off onto a country road, she meandered down a narrow road bisecting two vineyards, the ragged, tooth-like mountains now directly in front of her. Winter was just arriving in this pretty valley and the vines looked denuded, like tiny, old hunched men. Addi turned into an oak-tree-lined driveway—the trees would look magnificent in summer—and her eyebrows lifted as Jude's house came into view.

Instead of the Cape Dutch house she'd expected—the old, gracious houses that were dotted around the countryside like grand old dames—Jude's house was a modern, sprawling one-storey creation of glass, wood and steel. But somehow, despite being ruthlessly modern, it looked warm and welcoming and suited its surroundings. He must have had an incredibly talented architect as it was…dared she say it?… perfect. She adored the house and loved the big trees and wild garden running up to the edges of the vineyards.

She parked her car next to a brand-new SUV—top of the line, she noted, with all the bells and whistles—and wondered how Jude could reconcile his save-the-planet views with his gas-guzzling car. Tipping the rear-view mirror so she could see her reflection, she grimaced at her red eyes and sallow skin. Using her finger, she rubbed away dots of mascara and dug in her bag for some lipstick, hoping it would give her a bit of a lift. She stroked the bold red colour over her lips and winced. All it did was highlight her bloodshot eyes and gaunt face. Addi cursed and reached for a tissue to wipe it off but, before she could, she heard a knock on her window.

Jumping, she spun around to see a broad chest and mint-coloured jersey plastered against a flat stomach, a stomach she knew was ridged with hard muscle. As she'd discovered weeks ago, his body was phenomenal and his muscles had muscles of their own. He was sexy, powerful and masculine...

Okay, enough of that now. Addi gave herself a mental slap and Jude yanked open her car door.

'Are you coming in or what?' he demanded, sounding impatient.

'Hello to you too,' she muttered, reaching for her tote bag that held her laptop and a thick stack of reports she'd had Greg print off. She hadn't had time to do a presentation; she'd just have to wing it. Addi exited her car and tugged down her fitted jacket, shivering in the cool wind rolling down the mountain and across the vineyards. Clouds were building up in the distance, gathering cold raindrops.

Addi looked at the house and wished it was hers. She wished she was walking into it after a hard day, with Jude looking welcoming instead of threatening, ready with a hug or a cup of tea. She wished he was the man she could turn to, someone who'd help her make sense of the crazy, chaotic meeting at the lawyer's office, someone utterly and for ever on her side. For some reason, she could imagine Jude in that role, could almost feel those big arms wrapping her up, being the barrier between her and the world, his deep voice encouraging her, soothing her anxiety...

You might be attracted to Fisher, Addi, but

you are not looking for anything more! You don't believe in more!

Wow, she was either more upset or more tired than she'd thought, as she'd given up on fairy tales a long time ago. Prince Charming didn't exist, she didn't need anyone to rescue her; she'd sort herself out, thank you very much. People always disappointed her and there were no happy-ever-afters to be had. The best she could hope for was a 'happy for now', or for the immediate future.

Irritated with herself, she followed Jude to the enormous front door, impressed when he stepped back to let her enter the house in front of him. She turned around slowly, taking in the steel beams, the ultra-high ceilings and the slate floor. On the wall were bright abstract paintings in bold colours that were warm, interesting and, strangely, comforting.

She looked to her left, where the hallway flowed into a large open-plan kitchen, dining and living room. A large wooden table with bench seats separated the chef's kitchen from the living room, and comfortable-looking couches sat around a free-standing fireplace. But it was the view that caught and held her attention. Huge floor-to-ceiling windows ran from the kitchen area to the end of the lounge, allowing a one-eighty-degree view of the vineyards and the jagged mountain range beyond. The house was built on the edge of a slope and one level down was an impressive outdoor entertainment area and a huge pool, complete with Jacuzzi, at one end.

It was an impressive house, and it suited him, Addi thought.

'Coffee?' he asked, gesturing to the kitchen.

Ugh, no. She couldn't think of anything she wanted less. 'Water, please.'

He nodded, walked into the kitchen area and went to a brushed-steel fridge. He filled a glass before turning to his state-of-the-art coffee machine.

'Nice place,' Addi said, hanging onto her tote bag with a one-handed grip. 'I presume you are off the grid?'

He nodded. 'Totally.'

She couldn't help it, she needed to needle him, just a little. It was either that or step into his arms for a hug, and she couldn't do that. If he showed her any sympathy right now, she'd dissolve into a puddle. 'How do you reconcile your "environment first" views and your gas-guzzling car?'

He shoved a cup under the nozzle of the coffee machine and used the side of his hand to hit the start button, dispensing espresso into the tiny cup. The smell wafted over to Addi and she had to breathe through her mouth and swallow a couple of times. 'It's a hybrid, Addi. I try, as far as I possibly can, to run off electricity but sometimes that isn't always practical.'

She nodded, feeling a little foolish. She looked around. 'Where do you want to work?' she asked, wishing they could get on with it. She'd give him a run-down on the Thorpe assets and then she'd go home and spend the rest of the night trying to figure out how to tell him he was going to be a dad, and how to tell Lex that she'd messed up contraception-wise. And, most importantly, she needed time to research lawyers who specialised in family law, and hopefully get an idea as to how much they charged.

Blasted Joelle! How *dared* she?

Addi clenched her fists and jaw, trying to push away the anger. If she let it take hold, it would overwhelm her. If she cracked open the door to her emotions, despair and fear would sneak in and she'd be lost.

No, she had to keep it together. Thanks to having plenty of practice, keeping it together was what she did.

Addi looked awful, in the way that only a spectacularly gorgeous woman could.

Despite looking nothing like the glamourous woman in the slip dress he remembered from eight weeks ago—the one with the smoky eyes, the bold lips and the very kissable mouth—Jude's heart still kicked up a pace and the fabric of his trousers tightened. Then he looked closer, and concern replaced desire. Her eyes were road-map-red and puffy, and her nose looked a little pink. And, frankly, in her loose black trousers and slouchy jacket, she looked like a slight breeze could blow her away. She looked burned out and miserable, as if she needed a hot meal and a long hug.

Was she upset? Or sick?

He didn't think he was completely oblivious to the emotions of the women who briefly shared his bed, but neither had he dwelled on them the way he was now doing with Addi. He wanted to know why she was upset, whether she was okay and, terrifyingly, how he could fix whatever was worrying her. He wasn't a fix-it type of guy; he always kept his distance. So, what was it about this woman who tugged at the heartstrings he hadn't thought he had?

Walking over to her, he took her bag off her shoulder, surprised at the weight of it. Taking her cold hand, he led her over to the fireplace and dumped her bag on the closest chair. 'Take off your jacket and sit down before you collapse, Addi,' he told her, his tone suggesting she not argue. 'When last did you eat?'

She sank onto the couch but managed to glare at him. She opened her mouth, no doubt to ask him what business it was of his, but he lifted a hand to stop her snappy retort. 'I have chicken soup that's ready to be heated, as well as sourdough bread. You're going to have a bowl, and when you have some colour back in your cheeks we might, or might not, discuss business.'

She lifted her stubborn chin. 'I'm fine, Jude. And I have minimal time, so I can't waste it eating.'

Her words lacked fire and he was getting more worried by the second. What was wrong with her? He intended to find out. But, first, she needed food.

He placed his hands on his hips and cocked his head. 'Did that sound like a suggestion?' he asked. 'Because it wasn't. You will eat. We'll see where we go from there.'

When Addi didn't reply, he knew that he'd won this round. He didn't presume he'd win the next. Swallowing his frustrated sigh, he left her by the fire and walked back into the kitchen area. He pulled soup out of the fridge—his housekeeper was an amazing cook—and reached into a cupboard for a bowl. Looking back, he saw Addi scrabbling in her tote bag and shook his head when she pulled out her phone.

She started scrolling, her back hunched and her head drooping. It was so obvious she needed a break and looking at her phone wasn't going to allow her to de-stress.

'Addi.'

She didn't hear him, so he raised his voice and called her name again. She didn't acknowledge him; she was miles away, immersed in something on her phone. He walked into the utility room off the kitchen and cut the Internet connection. Thanks to being deep in a valley, all electronic contact came through a high-speed fibre connection, and he'd just killed the power to the modem.

Smiling to himself, he walked back into the kitchen, just in time to see Addi spinning around to glare at him. 'I've lost signal.'

Yep.

'I need to be connected,' she told him, sounding frantic.

No, she didn't. The world wouldn't stop turning if she wasn't plugged in for a couple of hours. He shrugged. 'The signal out here is iffy; it might come back on, or it might not.'

If she gave it any thought, she'd realise that he ran a multi-billion-dollar operation and needed to be constantly connected. He was banking on the fact she was too tired and too stressed to work that out. As he expected, her shoulders slumped and she tossed her phone onto the couch next to her.

'Lean back, kick off your shoes and stare at the mountain,' he told her. 'Breathe.'

Addi handed him another glare and turned her back on him. He put the bowl of soup into the microwave to heat up and, when he turned back to look at her, she'd done as he'd suggested—her feet were tucked under her bottom, and she had a cushion behind her head. She was also looking at the awesome view, watching the clouds skim over the mountain, blocking out the sun. It was going to storm later, and the temperature would drop. Winter was starting to come in the Cape, and the first of a series of cold fronts was rolling in.

'How long have you owned this property?' Addi asked, her voice drifting over to him.

He sliced the sourdough bread. 'I bought the land about ten years ago and the house was completed about three years ago.'

'Do you make wine?' she asked.

He smiled. No; he didn't have the patience or the knowledge. 'I lease the vines to a neighbour and he takes the harvest. He makes a rather good Shiraz.' 'Rather good', as in one of the best in the world. He considered offering Addi a glass and then remembered she had to drive home. Besides, wine on an empty stomach—a stomach he suspected hadn't seen a decent meal for a while—was never a good idea.

The microwave dinged and he pulled out her soup. 'Come on over here,' he told her, sliding the bowl onto a place mat on the other side of the island. Addi stood up and, without bothering to put her heels on, padded over to the island, the hems of her now too-long trousers dragging against his slate floors. She climbed up onto a stool and bent down to smell the soup, her eyes closing.

'It smells good,' she told him. 'It smells like Aunt Kate's soup.'

He pushed the wooden board holding the bread over to her. 'Who is Aunt Kate?' he asked, keeping his voice neutral. He knew that if he got too demanding her shield would go back up.

'Uh...she was a great-aunt. My sister Lex and I lived with her from the time I turned seventeen,' Addi explained, dipping her spoon into the soup.

She took a deep breath and lifted the spoon to her mouth as if she wasn't sure how she'd react. She swallowed, sighed and then dug in, rapidly lifting spoonful after spoonful to her mouth and taking greedy bites out of the bread.

Jude watched her eat, fascinated. It was almost as if he'd faded away and all she could focus on was the meal. His housekeeper Greta was a good cook, sure, and the soup was nice, but it wasn't worthy of her constant murmurs of appreciation.

When Addi scraped the last of the soup from the bowl and ate the last bite of bread, she looked up at him. Her cheeks were red. She looked embarrassed at diving in but at least she had some colour. Her eyes were a little brighter and some of the tension in her shoulders had eased.

She patted her stomach and sent him a shy smile. 'You have no idea how much I needed that,' she told him.

Oh, he did. He rested his forearms on the counter and frowned at her. 'Why haven't you been eating, Addi? What's Addi short for, by the way?' He'd been wondering about that, mostly late at night when X-rated memories of the way they'd loved each other bombarded him.

'Addison.'

He tasted her full name on his tongue and found he liked it. 'So, what gives? And don't tell me "nothing".'

She stared down at the empty soup bowl and lifted a hand to her hair to run her fingers through the bright blonde. They were trembling, and it annoyed him. What was she scared of?

'Talk to me, Addison,' he commanded. She had the weight of the world on her shoulders, and he suspected that if she didn't talk to someone soon that weight might just flatten her. He'd tried to push away his need to help her, to get involved, but every time he did it came roaring back, stronger than before. This woman could turn him inside out and he wasn't enjoying the very alien sensation.

Addi cocked her head and tried to smile but it hardly lifted the corners of her lips and didn't reach her eyes. 'Are you sure you want to know, Jude?'

He wouldn't have asked if he didn't, as he told her.

'People say that, but when they hear the unexpected they tend to shoot the messenger,' Addi murmured.

'I've been around for a long time, Addi, and I'm not easily shocked,' Jude assured her. 'And sometimes it's helpful to get another person's input.'

Addi didn't look convinced. She picked up her spoon and tapped it against the rim of the bowl, obviously agonising over her decision to speak or not. He wanted her to, he realised. There was something about this prickly woman that made him want to pull her in, hold her close and be the barrier between the world and her. He felt protective of her, and he couldn't understand why. The women he normally dated—or slept with; calling what they did together 'dating' was a stretch—were independent and successful, women who neither needed nor wanted his protection and would laugh if he suggested it. But Addi, stubborn and guarded, looked as if she needed it.

He removed the spoon from her hand and stopped the annoying *ting-ting-ting* of her spoon hitting the bowl. Addi looked surprised and he realised that she hadn't even noticed the noise. She'd been too busy deciding whether to talk or how to frame her words.

Cold fear ran up and down his spine. Was she ill? Had she done something illegal? Was she in trouble? Seriously, if she didn't start to speak in the next five minutes, he might just shake it out of her.

'Where do I start?' she asked, her words a rhetorical question. She looked away from him and out of the window, her eyes focused on the vines outside. 'I'm worried about not having a job when Cole sells up Thorpe Industries. The new owners of the hospitality division might not want to take me on and a severance package only goes so far.'

He'd looked her up online. She had an excellent degree and great experience; he doubted she'd battle to find another job. 'I need my job. I've got expenses and people relying on me,' she added.

'Who?' he asked. He knew she was single, so who was she supporting?

'I live with three half-sisters,' she told him.

'Lex is a year younger than me, and she looks after our two younger sisters. Lex is also studying towards her degree. Our youngest half-sisters are six and eight. Mine is the salary that keeps us afloat.'

Jude rubbed his jaw, taking in her words. He had so many questions and didn't know where to start. Where were her parents, all their parents? Why was she looking after her half-sisters? 'Wait, let me get this right—you have three sisters?'

This time her smile reached her eyes. 'I have four, actually. Storm is our middle sister, but she doesn't live with us. She's twenty-four and has a job as an au pair. She, thank God, is financially independent.'

Right. She had *four* sisters. Wow.

He pulled his thoughts back to her initial statement. 'You should be able to pick up another job, Addi. I can't see why you wouldn't.'

She closed her eyes briefly. 'Do you remember that I told you that I couldn't be here at two o'clock because I had an appointment with a lawyer?'

Since the conversation had only been this morning, of course he remembered. She'd said it was a personal issue. 'Yes.'

'The appointment was regarding custody of my younger sisters. I was informed earlier that my flaky mother wants Snow and Nixi back. After four years away, she wants to take them to live with her in India. She's been living in Thailand for the past fifteen years. I have to think that there's a man involved…there's always a man involved whenever Joelle makes a life-changing decision.'

Right; that was unexpected.

'I need to find a family lawyer who can help me sue for custody of my sisters. I will not let them be uprooted again and I will not put them through the unstable life Lex and I endured. But to gain custody of them I'd need both a lawyer and a job—a guaranteed source of income to pay for said lawyer.'

'As I said, you shouldn't have a problem picking up a good job.' What was he missing here?

'I presume you've heard about pregnancy discrimination?'

Of course he had. Along with believing in equal pay for women doing the same work as men, he didn't believe in treating a pregnant employee unfavourably. But why were they talking about pregnancy discrimination?

'By the time I get round to looking for a new job, when I'm ready to attend interviews, I will be showing. While it's against the law for my pregnancy to be used as a reason not to hire me, we all know it happens and it's incredibly difficult to prove, especially if several decent candidates apply for the job.'

But what did that have to do with…? Oh. *Right*. 'You're pregnant?' he asked, rubbing his chin.

She tipped her head to one side and nodded, her eyebrows raised. 'I found out this morning.'

He was finding it difficult to connect the dots, to work out why her eyebrows were still raised, why she was looking at him with that 'come on, catch up' expression on her face.

Addi looked him in the eye and sucked in a deep breath. 'I don't know how it happened, Jude, but you're the father of my baby.'

CHAPTER FOUR

IT WAS DONE. There was no going back now.

Addi slid off her seat, walked over to the floor-to-ceiling window and placed her hand on the glass, staring past her reflection to look out onto the almost dark garden. The occasional raindrop splattered against the door and the temperature outside had plummeted.

It didn't feel too toasty in here either.

She'd dumped a lot of information on Jude, and he needed time to think about what she'd said, time to work through the bombshell she'd dropped. She normally never allowed her mouth to run away with her, she always considered her words, but something about Jude Fisher had made her throw caution to the wind and she'd spilt all her drama. She didn't like it.

Obtaining custody of Nixi and Snow wasn't his problem, and she'd sort herself out work-wise. All he had to wrap his head around was the fact that he was going to be a father. Whether he played a role in the baby's life was up to him. She wouldn't force him to. She'd grown up with a father who'd only contacted her on high days and holidays—and sometimes didn't even bother to do that—so she knew her baby would be fine with not having a father in her, or his, life. She'd turned out okay, hadn't she? Kids were resilient, far more so than people imagined.

Behind her, Jude cleared his throat, and Addi turned to look at him, resting her palms flat on the glass behind her. The windows, as she discovered, were actually doors and could slide into one another, opening up the entire house to the elements. Right now, she wished they'd open up so she could fall into the night. She really didn't want to continue this conversation. She'd eaten, was feeling washed out and she could sleep for a week.

She genuinely didn't know how she was going to find the energy to drive home.

'You're pregnant?'

She nodded.

'And it's mine?'

She lifted her chin at the note of disbelief she heard in his voice. 'Well, since I haven't slept with anyone else but you for years, I'd say the chances were high.' She winced, wishing she didn't default to sarcasm when she felt off balance.

Jude didn't look as though he appreciated her attitude either. 'We used *condoms*, Addison. Every time.'

Addi pushed a hand into her hair and tugged at the short strands. 'I don't know how to explain it, Jude, but one of them must've had a tear or a hole or something.'

'I've been using condoms for too many years to count and I've never had so much as a scare,' Jude told her, folding his arms across his chest.

She saw something flash in his eyes and frowned. Why did she think that something about his statement wasn't true? It didn't matter; they were dealing with the here and now, not the past.

'I don't know what to say, or how to explain how it happened,' Addi replied, her voice creeping up in volume.

'Are you sure you are…?'

'Of course I'm sure! I've missed my period and I did three tests, Jude! I'm not making this up, I haven't made a mistake and I wish I wasn't!

'I don't want to be pregnant, Jude, I wish I was anything but pregnant because it complicates my life exponentially. It complicates my job situation; it might complicate getting custody of my half-sisters. It will definitely put a strain on what is already a difficult family set-up. I do *not* want to be pregnant but I am. And I have to deal with it.'

Jude walked over to the lounge area and dropped to sit on the closest couch. He rested his forearms on his knees and lowered his head, looking as though she'd sideswiped him with a baseball bat.

She walked over to him and sat down next to him, keeping a foot between him. 'I thought you should know, that's all.'

He took a while to respond and when he lifted his head his eyes were granite-hard and a flat, dark green. The man who'd looked so concerned earlier had morphed into a ruthless businessman.

'Okay, so what do you want, Addison?' he demanded, leaning back and placing an ankle on the opposite knee. It was a casual stance, but she knew that he was a harnessed tornado, ready to touch down and create havoc. 'A job? A cash pay-out? *What?*'

Addi stared at him, not knowing where his fierce words were coming from. She didn't want money and hadn't asked for a job. She'd just thought he needed to know, that he had the right to know. She wouldn't even expect him to pay child support, because if a flake like Joelle could raise her two oldest daughters without receiving a bean from either of their two fathers, she could too. She was smart and resourceful and she'd do it on her own, without input from anyone.

She relied on herself. Always. And she was tired of this conversation, exhausted by the events of the day. She wanted to go home, have a warm bath and climb into bed with a cup of hot chocolate. But first she had to make the drive home.

And, the sooner she got started on that, the better.

Addi stood up, slipped her feet back into her heels and picked up her jacket from where she'd draped it over the back of the chair earlier. She removed the thick print-out from her tote bag and slammed it onto the wooden coffee table. Jude could whistle if she thought she'd spend another minute in his company discussing hotels. In a couple of days, she'd have to face him again—she still had a job to do—but for now she needed time and space. They both did.

After digging her car keys out of the side pocket of her tote bag, she pulled her bag over her shoulder and walked to the front door, leaving Jude where he was. He didn't deserve a goodbye, he'd chosen to believe the worst of her. Making a buck and working an angle was something Joelle did, not her. She might look like her mother, but she tried to be as little like her personality-wise as possible.

She'd sort this out herself, forge her own path and plough through it. She was better off on her own. She always had been.

It took Jude ten minutes to make sense of what Addi had been trying to say, another five to realise she'd left his house.

He couldn't believe that this was happening to him. This was his worst nightmare. Apart from the fact that he was freaked out that his mum had died because of a pregnancy—what if that happened to Addi?—he was once again, after sixteen years, talking to a woman about her being pregnant, trying to make sense of her words.

Jude placed his elbows on his knees and his head in his hands, memory after sour memory rolling in. He'd met Marina at university a few weeks into his second year, and she'd been the first woman to capture his heart. He'd been ridiculously, crazily in love with her, and he'd danced to her tune. Marina's friends had become his, he'd neglected his studies and he'd pulled away from his friends. She'd been all that was important, all he'd been able to think about.

She'd also single-handedly caused him more problems than anyone before or since. Admittedly, he'd been a spoiled student, one of the wealthiest at the upmarket university, and had had unlimited spending power thanks to the credit card his grandfather had handed him. He'd driven a soft top, been good-looking and, yeah, he'd been the big man on campus. Perfect bait for the money-and-status-hungry Marina.

She'd looked like a doll, dark-haired and dark-eyed, and had barely weighed a hundred pounds. But she was possibly the smartest woman he'd ever encountered—street-smart, not book-smart—and she'd seen him coming. Used to girls falling over him, it had taken him six weeks to get her to notice him and another month to get her to agree to a date. The adage 'treat 'em mean and keep 'em keen' had worked on him, and he'd revelled in the chase, thinking he would win the biggest prize.

Soon after they'd started sleeping together, he'd decided she was the woman he'd marry, the future mother of his kids, his for-ever life partner. His parents had died when he'd been a kid and his grandfather, Bartholomew Fisher, had obtained custody of him. With Bart being a workaholic, he'd had a lonely and isolated upbringing. Boarding school had been a life saver, and when he'd gone to his school friends' homes for the weekends and holidays he'd discovered real families, noise and laughter, teasing and the affection. He'd wanted that, with all the desperation of a lonely kid, lost and lacking in affection, could.

His grandfather had been a hard, impatient

man, one who hadn't accepted foibles and failures. They were Fishers, and they had higher standards than most, and Jude was expected to exceed those standards. He'd had to be academically successful, a good sportsman—luckily for him, he was better than average—and socially charming. Fishers were gentlemen—they said and did the right thing. Or, more importantly, were *seen* to do the right thing. Bart had blithely told him he had mistresses, he occasionally cut legal and financial corners and he didn't shy away from a dodgy deal—the trick was not to get caught. And Fishers never aired their dirty linen in public.

Like Jude, Marina didn't have a family—she'd been raised by an elderly aunt and she'd attended university on a scholarship. He'd been a rich kid, she'd been a poor girl, but they had been what the other needed. Or so he'd thought.

While he'd been planning their life together, she'd been planning something totally different. Unknown to Jude, Marina had contacted Bartholomew and demanded a substantial amount of money for her to disappear from his life. If he didn't pay up, she would accuse Jude of coercing her into a relationship and claim she was pregnant.

Bart had rolled into the university town on a cloud of black smoke and brimstone and accused

him of being the stupidest creature in the history
of the world. Reeling at the barrage of information, Jude had listened, stunned, as he was told
of the blackmail attempt. Bart had had his 'people'—private investigators, Jude assumed—do
some digging and it had turned out that wasn't
the first time Marina had put her hooks into a
wealthy student—she'd done it at the University
of Johannesburg and at the University of Cape
Town. Bart had told him that she wasn't nineteen, like Jude, but twenty-five and was an old
hand at scams.

Rocked to his core, but in love, he'd defended
Marina and had told his grandfather he was
wrong, that he was mistaken. Being young, dumb
and far too proud, he'd chosen to stick by Marina. In retaliation, Bartholomew had cut off his
allowance. Too proud to go and ask for money
from his cold, unfeeling and harsh relative, he'd
found a job as a bar tender at a popular club to
meet Marina's and his bills.

He'd been confident and desperately naive:
they loved each other and they could make this
work if they pulled together—if Marina got a
job. But working for a living was not what she'd
wanted, and it became clear if Jude couldn't get
his grandfather to reinstate his allowance she'd
be out of there. He'd refused—the very first time

he'd refused her anything—and had left for his bar-tending shift.

He'd returned home around one-thirty that same night to find her awake, sitting cross-legged on the bed. She'd told him she was pregnant and had opened her hand, revealing a pill. She'd told him she would abort his baby unless he arranged for her to receive a substantial pay-out. She'd said, if he couldn't give her the life she wanted, then she wasn't going to give birth and raise a child she didn't want—there were other guys out there who could give her what she wanted and deserved.

Two things happened that night, almost instantaneously. The scales fell from Jude's eyes and Jude realised she'd never loved him and he'd been just another mark. He knew instinctively that she wasn't pregnant and, when he called her bluff, she shrugged and told him the lie was worth the shot.

After kicking her out of his flat—at that point he didn't care where she went or what she did—he sat on his shower floor. He'd had a couple of moments of sheer terror before his brain had kicked in, and he vowed that he would never again allow a woman to put him in that untenable position. He would be ultra-careful about protecting against unwanted pregnancy and he'd never allow a woman to trap him again.

It took another eighteen months, and a stint at the London School of Economics, for him to mend fences with his grandfather. But there was always a barrier between them—a lack of communication, and on Bart's part a distinct lack of trust. Jude took his place at Fisher International, but Bart made a habit of looking over his shoulder and double-checking his every move.

Jude put up with it, knowing that dealing with his irascible grandfather was a small price to pay to inherit the company he truly loved. As the years passed, the sting and embarrassment of Marina's treachery passed too and he started dating again, and even flirted with the idea of living with, and perhaps eventually marrying, a British banker called Jane. That idea was kiboshed when he discovered she had flexible views on fidelity, and he called it quits.

What he didn't expect was for her to spill his story about being scammed by Marina—told to her under the influence of too many whiskies—to one of her friends working on Fleet Street. Thank God he hadn't told her about the fake pregnancy threat because that would've made the papers too.

Was it any wonder he had difficulty trusting anyone?

Bartholomew abhorred the negative publicity and raked him over the coals for being an idiot, embarrassing him and revealing family secrets. He died about three months after the tabloid article was first published and Jude discovered he'd amended his will the day after the story broke. Fisher International would still be his but, because Bart couldn't trust his judgement, all major Fisher International decisions had to be approved by a board of trustees for ten years. But Bart hadn't stopped there: if Jude fathered a child out of wedlock, or was involved in any more scandals that might tarnish the Fisher name, the trustees would remain in place for another ten years.

He was so close to being free, to being able to run his company the way he wanted to. But if Addi gave birth to his child, and the trustees were presented with that information, he would be constrained and hamstrung for another ten years. He couldn't do it; he couldn't allow the Council of Three to have the final say for another decade.

There was only one thing he could do.

Addi pulled into her space under the steel carport adjacent to her house and sat in her car, watching the rain fall in a steady sheet. It was bucketing down now, and the storm had followed her all the way home. She shuddered as a bolt of lightning lit up the sky, quickly followed by deep, rolling thunder. It would storm and then it would drizzle for days.

Winter was well and truly on the way.

Addi looked at the house and knew she should go inside, listen to Nixi and Snow ramble about their day and be a good sister. But, after the day she'd had, she felt depleted. She didn't even have the energy to feel guilty about not wanting to be with them right now. If she knew she wouldn't freeze, she'd curl up in her car seat and go to sleep.

She was tired on a whole new level.

Addi heard a knock on her window and jumped, whipping her head round to see her sister's freckled face on the other side of the window. Lex wrapped her arms around her slim torso and bounced up and down, raindrops glistening on her red curls.

As soon as the window dropped, Lex spoke. 'What on earth are you doing, Ads? You've been out here for ages!'

Had she? She hadn't realised. 'Hey, Lex.'

Lex frowned at her. 'Are you okay? You look terrible.'

Fantastic. Addi nodded, sighed and wondered whether she should invite Lex into the car and tell her the entire story. Lex was not only her sister but also her best friend and they'd been a team all of their lives. They were in this together. But telling Lex that she was pregnant was so much harder than she thought it would be. They'd promised each other that they'd be radically over-cautious about protection, that they'd never bring an unwanted child into the world.

That they wouldn't, in any way, follow in Joelle's footsteps.

But here she was…

And by falling pregnant she'd jeopardised her job, their income and perhaps their continued, albeit casual, custody of the girls. If Joelle's lawyer used the argument that Addi had her own child to look after and raise, and that she couldn't give the girls all the financial and emotional support they needed, a judge might think they'd be better off with their mum.

And, while she really wanted to share her burdens with Lex, she couldn't—not just yet. She needed to have a plan first, to know where she was going, before she told her sister the trio of bad news. If she had a plan, she could cope. Without one, she'd flounder.

'Am I coming in there or are you coming into the house?' Lex demanded.

'I'll be there in a sec, Lex, let me grab my stuff.'

Lex nodded. Addi reached for the tote bag and her phone fell to the floor. She picked it up and saw that she had a dozen missed calls and text messages. Strange, because she hadn't heard any of them come through.

She fiddled with her settings and realised that she'd somehow put her phone on silent. Scrolling through the messages, she saw that they were all from Jude…

We need to talk.

The storm is really bad. Are you okay?

Dammit, Addi, I know you were upset when you left but can you please let me know if you are okay? There's flooding on the road you're on…

Right, that's it. I'm coming to look for you.

Addi widened her eyes at his increasingly irate and worried texts. She was a big girl, had been looking after herself and Lex since her teens, and didn't need any man checking up on her.

Will you please call me?

But the last thing she needed was another dust-up with Jude; she couldn't handle any more tonight. Pulling up his contact number, she told Lex she was just going to make a quick call, when headlights swung into their driveway. Addi turned around in her seat and immediately recognised the huge car sitting on the other side of the gate. She released a loud groan.

'Ads, there's a strange car in our driveway,' Lex stated.

Addi scrambled out of the car and placed a reassuring hand on her shoulder. 'It's fine, Lex, I know who it is.' Addi hit the button on her remote control, the gate slid open and Jude drove onto their property.

Lex turned to look at her, her red eyebrows lifting. 'And who might that be?'

'Jude Fisher. He's a…' How did she explain him? The man who'd rocked her world? The guy with whom she'd created a baby? The star of all her sexy dreams? 'He's someone I'm working with.'

'And why is he at our house at eight on a Wednesday night?' Lex asked, her eyebrows lifting even further as Jude parked behind Addi's car.

'Good question,' Addi murmured as Jude left his car and half-walked, half-ran through the driving rain to join them under the car port.

He stared at her, his eyes running over her body, and she saw him release a sigh. 'You're okay.'

Addi nodded. 'I am.' She saw his expression

harden and anger flash in his eyes, but before he could blast her—because she knew he wanted to—she turned to Lex. 'Lex, this is Jude Fisher. Jude, my sister, Lex.'

Jude nodded at Lex, and her sister's eyes bounced between the big man who'd unexpectedly rocked up at their house and Addi.

'I need to talk to Jude, Lex,' Addi told her. 'I'll come in soon.'

Lex looked as if she was about to invite Jude inside, but Addi shook her head and Lex caught the tiny gesture. Her sister, no wallflower, just folded her arms. 'Will you be okay with him out here on your own?'

Addi nodded. She wasn't scared of Jude; she knew he would never harm her. They might yell and shout—and that was why she wasn't going to invite him into the house—but he'd never use his strength or power to physically hurt her. 'I'm fine, Lex, I won't be long.'

Lex stared at Jude, her eyes narrowing, and finally walked away. Addi knew that she'd stand just inside the back door, just far enough away to give them privacy. The sisters looked out for one another.

Addi turned back to Jude, who'd pulled on a black cashmere jersey over his open-neck shirt. 'What are you doing here, Fisher?' she asked.

He put his hands on his hips and glared down at

her. 'When I came out of my "I'm having a baby" shock, you were gone, and about five minutes later there was a cloudburst. I couldn't get hold of you and I went online to see social media blowing up with posts about flooding on the road you were driving on. Gale-force winds also pushed cars off the road. There were multiple accidents and, when you didn't reply, I thought you were in one.'

He looked genuinely frightened. 'I was ahead of the storm, just,' she told him.

'Look, I know that my response wasn't ideal—'

'You accused me of trying to scam you!' Addi replied, her tone turning hot.

He dragged his hand through his damp hair. 'But when you didn't reply I thought something had happened to you.'

She lifted her shoulders and looked away. 'That would be convenient, right?'

His big hands grabbed her shoulders and he bent his knees so that their eyes were level. His sparked with angry green fire. 'Don't ever say that to me again, okay?'

Addi frowned, confused, because he not only sounded angry but also genuinely upset. She wasn't sure what was happening here, and she felt as though she was holding a script but couldn't read the words. Looking down, she pulled her bottom lip between her teeth before speaking again.

'I'm sorry I didn't answer, my phone was on silent, and I didn't hear any of your calls or messages. I was about to call you when I saw your headlights lighting up my house.'

He looked as though he wanted to argue but, instead of doing that, he dragged in another long breath and yanked her to him, holding her against his hard body. Despite not wanting to, despite telling herself that she had to be strong and keep her spine straight, she sagged against him, resting her temple against his collar bone and letting his heat envelop her. He was so warm and so solid, so damn capable. He felt like a barrier between the world and her, a place she could rest, where she could *be*. Silly, but for a moment, just one or two, she wanted to lean in, to soak in his strength—something she never did.

It wasn't her way, but how wonderful it would be to be looked after, not to feel so alone, so responsible, to be the one everyone relied on for everything. To be in a partnership, a give-and-take. But dreams were for fools, and she'd never been offered the time, space or opportunity to be foolish.

His hand held the back of her head, his fingers massaging her scalp. 'You've had a bit of a day, haven't you?'

'Yes,' she agreed. She pulled back to look up at him. 'So, to be fair, did you.'

He almost smiled.

'The soup was good,' she told him, wanting to lighten the atmosphere between them. She knew she should pull away and put some distance between them. But, before she could find the will to do that, he lifted his hand to touch her cheek, his thumb gliding over her cheekbone and then over her bottom lip.

Addi held her breath, knowing that sharing a kiss would be stupid—she was working for him, with him, they were going to have a child together and they had things to discuss—but she didn't care. His kisses and touch had the ability to take her away, to make her forget that it was a cold, rainy night and that her life was currently the emotional equivalent of a storm surge.

His mouth met hers and, like before, heat skittered through her, desire on its heels. Jude nibbled at her mouth, his soft touch more erotic than she remembered, and she couldn't help closing the gap between them, pushing her breasts into his chest and trying to hold as much of his broad back as possible. She felt the dip of his spine beneath his clothes and told herself that she couldn't, shouldn't, slide her hand up and under, looking for bare skin.

But her body decided to ignore her brain and she sighed when she felt his warm, bare skin under her cool hands. Her mouth opened, Jude's tongue slid inside, and stress faded away. There was only his warm mouth, his minty but masculine taste, and his bare hand sliding up her ribcage and over her lace-covered breast to find her nipple. He tipped her head to the side, seeking deeper access to her mouth, his tongue twisting around hers. Addi slipped her thigh between his, needing to get closer, wanting her feminine core against his hard erection. Nobody had ever made her feel so out of control…

She was just a few feet from her back door, and a few doors down was her bedroom…

Jude pulled away, released a curse and moved his hands back to her shoulders, putting a few feet between them. The sound of his ragged breathing filled the space between them and she felt adrift, as if she'd been wrenched from a lovely, sexy dream and drop-kicked back into reality.

She didn't like it.

Jude dropped his hands and took another step back, creating more distance between them. From inside the house, she could hear Lex talking to the girls and the sound of their ancient washing machine. The next-door neighbour's dog released a series of yippy barks. Addi didn't know how life could carry on like normal around them. When Jude had kissed her, she'd felt something move in the universe, as though there was a crack in the night sky, that a black hole had formed and sucked her into it.

But wasn't that all airy-fairy and terribly woo-woo for a practical, down-to-earth girl like herself? She needed to stop thinking and feeling like that—immediately.

She rubbed her hand over her face and fought the urge to ask what that kiss had meant, where they went from here to put plans in place. She felt uneasy and turned on, a completely horrible combination.

Jude ran his hand over his jaw. 'I'm glad you're safely home, Addison.'

Addi looked at him, waiting for more. That was it? That was all he was going to say?

He nodded at his car. 'I'm going to go.'

He was going? But they had things to discuss and plans to make. He couldn't just walk away.

Before she could say anything, he held up his hand. 'Addi, I can see the words on your tongue—a million questions, even more ideas. Let's park it for now, okay? I need to think; you do too. We've argued, we've kissed, we've had life-changing news. I think we need to let it settle before we go into the ifs, whys and hows.'

That sounded sensible, but Addi didn't want to be sensible, she wanted a plan. Now. Tonight. She felt in control when she had a plan and liked knowing where she was going and what her next steps needed to be.

'But...'

He shook his head. 'Have a bath, get an early night. Try to chill. We'll talk soon.'

Chill—he thought she could *chill*? Had that kiss scrambled his brains? 'I'm not a *chilled* type of person.'

A smile hit his mouth, then his eyes. 'I gathered that. But nothing will change overnight, nothing *can*. So, maybe just give yourself a break and allow me time to catch up.'

He was right—spending the night worrying and running scenarios wouldn't change anything between now and tomorrow. She'd try to relax, but she doubted she could, as she told Jude.

'I'll talk to you soon, Addison,' he told her, moving closer to her to drop a kiss on her temple. 'We'll work something out.'

His reassurance was just four words—we'll work something out—but it made her feel as though she wasn't alone, as though she had someone standing by her side. Maybe she was being overly optimistic, because his kiss had scrambled her brain, but she felt calmer, less panicky and able to get a bit more air into her lungs.

But, as Jude walked to his car, she told herself to stop conning herself. People routinely let her down, and she must have rocks in her head if she thought that Jude Fisher would be any different.

Around the corner, Jude wrenched his steering wheel to the left, stopped his car, rested his thumping head on the steering wheel and tried to regulate his breathing.

He'd had a completely horrendous ninety minutes, every moment of which had been filled with visions of Addi's car being swept off the road, of her being hurt or possibly dead. When he hadn't been able to reach her, he hadn't stopped to think—he'd simply run out of his house, thrown himself into his car and belted down the slippery dirt road to the motorway. He'd kept his eyes peeled for a white hatchback, his heart in his mouth whenever he saw the flashing blue lights of an emergency vehicle. He'd never felt so helpless in his entire life—not a fun experience.

Jude pulled in his first proper breath, one that actually sent air to his lungs and oxygen to his brain. He'd been operating on fear and adrenalin for the last little while and he felt utterly wrecked.

He was a fit guy, but he felt as if he'd just completed the Comrades Marathon, and as out of breath and exhausted as when he'd run over that finish line five years ago. He felt shattered.

Jude lifted his head and released the tight grip on the steering wheel. He flexed his fingers and rolled his head, trying to loosen some of the knots in his neck.

Addi was fine, she was safe. He could just sit here and breathe. Her pregnancy news had shocked him, of course it had, but he'd been off-balance since she had stepped out of her car and onto his property. She was a potent mixture of spiky and vulnerable, and there was something about her that made him want to protect her, to pull her into his arms and be the barrier between the world and her.

He didn't know why, because she'd made it very clear that she didn't need him in any way, shape or form. With any other woman, that would have been a relief, but with Addi? Well, the craziness, of what she made him feel, was that he wanted her to turn to him, to lean on him a little, to allow him to carry some of the load she lugged around. He felt superfluous and deeply frustrated.

She still desired him—her hot, responsive kiss had made that very clear—but she wouldn't let herself need him. She was an independent woman, courageous, and, while he cursed her stubbornness, he appreciated her determination. She was tough, mentally and emotionally.

He admired that.

He respected her gutsiness. And he wanted her more now than ever.

Yep, he was lusting over the mother of his unborn child. Could he have made the situation more complicated if he'd tried? He didn't think so.

CHAPTER FIVE

ADDI SMOOTHED DOWN her cranberry-coloured swing dress and checked her thigh-high suede boots for watermarks. She wore solid black tights and a cream-coloured coat, accessorising with a green, scarlet-and-cream scarf.

For this meeting with Jude, she wanted to look something other than the pale, haggard creature he'd encountered at his house, so she'd taken a lot of care with her make-up, making her now thankfully clear blue eyes bigger and her mouth softer. She wanted to look successful, someone who had her life together, who had a plan…

She didn't have a plan.

Addi walked into the lobby of Fisher International's new headquarters and inhaled the smell of varnish and fresh paint. Jude had been caught up in the move for the past few days and she hadn't seen or spoken to him since they'd kissed four days ago.

But this morning she'd got a text message

from him, asking her to meet him at ten. Assuming it was a business meeting, she'd packed her laptop, run off another set of spreadsheets and made her way to the Waterfront.

The receptionist, big, buff and with flashing white teeth, handed her a security pass and gestured her to the bank of lifts on the other side of the lobby. 'The far lift door will open—that's Mr Fisher's private lift. It'll take you straight up to him.'

Addi tried to look as though she wasn't impressed by the private lift, but she was. Normally she ran up and down the steps of Thorpe Industries, partly to get some exercise but mostly because there were too few lifts to service the building, and she hated feeling like a trapped sardine.

Addi waited in front of the lift, removed her floppy black felt hat and ran her hand over her hair. It lay flat against her head today; she was channelling Audrey Hepburn and she knocked the hat against her thigh. She was nervous and she didn't like feeling that way.

She was only going to see the father of her burgeoning baby, the man who was going to buy the Thorpe assets and put her out of a job. What was there to be nervous about?

The lift doors opened and Addi stepped inside. There were no buttons and within seconds the lift door closed and she was shooting up. Her phone chimed with a message and she glanced down at the screen. It was a text message from her mother's lawyer, requesting a follow-up meeting.

She really needed to find a lawyer—one she could afford.

'One of these days, you're going to greet me with a smile, not a frown.'

Addi's head shot up. Jude stood on the other side of the lift door, looking suave in a very pale pink shirt, grey, metallic-silver tie and dark-grey trousers. He hadn't shaved and his stubble was a little heavy, a bit disreputable, and she liked the look.

Addi tucked her phone away and walked into his chaotic office. A plastic-covered couch sat in the corner, behind a stack of boxes and to the side of a massive desk. What she recognised as a brutally expensive leather chair sat on the other side of the desk. She realised Jude's back would be to the incredible view of the Waterfront Harbour and Signal Hill while he was working.

'Why did you put your desk there?' she demanded.

'I tried to work facing the view, but I was constantly distracted,' Jude replied. He gestured to the stack of boxes. 'Sorry it's a mess, we're still trying to get set up.'

Addi took a seat in the visitor's chair he offered and crossed one leg over the other, a little pleased when Jude's eyes lingered on the gap of her thigh between her boot and the hem of her short dress. A sexy memory from the night they spent together flashed and made her squirm and burn. His eyes collided with hers and she knew he was thinking of that night too. Was he remembering the way she'd straddled him, leaning down to kiss his mouth as she'd sheathed him? Or was he thinking about how he'd dropped to his knees in the shower and kissed her between her legs?

Whoa, boy.

Addi lifted her chin and told herself to get a grip. They were here to talk business…why else would he have asked her to meet at his office in the city?

Addi heard the door open behind her and she turned to see a handsome man enter, a tiny espresso cup in one hand and a clear mug holding what she thought might be tea.

The man flashed a grin at her and placed the mug in front of her. 'It's ginger-flavoured tea—I hope that's okay?'

'That's great, thank you,' she said, returning his smile. 'I'm Addi, by the way.'

'Thabo,' the man replied, handing Jude his

cup. 'I'm Jude's right hand. And his left. He pretty much can't function without me.'

Jude rolled his eyes. 'That's pretty accurate, actually. But don't be fooled—I make his coffee more often than he makes mine and, having a doctorate in business science, he's the guy I listen to. He's more a partner than an employee, and my closest confidant,' he told Addi. He leaned back, picked up his cup and sipped before looking at Thabo again. 'All organised?'

'Pretty much. I just need your go-ahead,' Thabo answered, sounding enigmatic. 'While you're away, our assistants can sort out your office and mine.'

Was Jude going away? When? Where to? And why did the thought of him leaving make her feel as though she had a boulder in her stomach and it was about to crash to the floor?

Thabo picked up a folder from Jude's desk and tapped it to his forehead in a salute. 'I'll leave you two to talk.'

Addi waited for him to leave the room before asking Jude whether Thabo knew she was pregnant. 'No, not yet. I'm still coming to terms with it myself.'

She gestured to the mug of hot tea.

'Uh, no. I saw your reaction to the smell of coffee when I made myself a cup the other day, and I assumed you might be feeling a bit off-colour with morning sickness. According to Dr Internet, ginger tea helps, supposedly, so I asked my assistant to get some in. Thabo probably just picked up the cups I asked her to make to save her a trip.'

He was not only observant but thoughtful. Addi felt his eyes on her, a little quizzical, a lot hot, and dragged her eyes off his gorgeous face to look past his shoulder to the wet and wild day happening outside. Storms were battering the Cape and nobody, least of all the meteorologists, knew when they'd see the sun again. It was predicted that the Cape would soon experience the wettest and coldest winter in decades, and she was not looking forward to it. She hated winter.

Addi picked up her mug, sipped and knew she was delaying the inevitable. She needed to know why Jude had asked her for this meeting.

'Am I here to talk you through Thorpe assets or are we going to talk about the baby?' she asked, thinking that being forthright was the best way to go. There was no point in tiptoeing around the subject; they needed to pull it out into the light.

And then pull it apart.

Jude nodded and linked his hands across his flat stomach. 'Either…both.'

Okay, then. 'Where do you want to start?' she asked.

'When are you due?' he asked, picking up a fountain pen and twisting it between his fingers.

'I've worked it out to be the end of the year,' she replied. 'They'll be able to give me more accurate due dates when I go for my first scan.'

'And when is that?' Jude asked.

Ah, she hadn't thought that far. She supposed she should, as soon as possible. 'I don't know. I need to find a doctor and make an appointment.'

'Do that,' Jude told her, and she felt steel slide into her spine. But she wouldn't call him out on his bossiness; she didn't want to start fighting with him ten minutes into their meeting.

'Yes, sir,' she muttered, unable to keep the sarcastic comment behind her teeth.

Jude smiled. 'You don't like being told what to do, do you?'

'Not even a little bit,' she admitted. 'Old Man Thorpe hired me out of university, I reported to him and he left me to my own devices. I only checked in with him when I had a problem. And, at home, in most ways I've been in charge for most of my life and I'm the one who gets things done, who paves the way, who makes the calls. I'm the oldest, so I took responsibility.'

'How old were you when you first started feeling like that?' Jude asked, looking interested.

Addi had to think back. 'Seven? Eight? I remember taking Joelle's bank card out of her purse and going to the cash machine. I went straight to the store and bought food—hot dogs, I think it was.'

'And what did your mother say about that?' Jude demanded, looking shocked.

'Joelle has a very fluid grasp on money, even less of what went into and out of her account,' she told him, before waving her hand. 'Why are we discussing my spacy mother?'

'I find you, your past and your family, interesting,' Jude told her. *Did he? Really? Why?* She supposed it was because she was totally different from the women he normally dated or was seen with. Unlike them, she didn't come from a 'good' family, and she wasn't rich, sophisticated, elegant or into art, poetry and opera.

'I think we should get married.'

Addi looked at him over the rim of her tea cup and, conscious of her shaking hand, slowly lowered the cup to the desk, trying not to spill her tea on his brand-new, expensive-looking carpet.

No, he couldn't possibly have said that, could he?

'I'm sorry, I thought you said that we should get married.'

Leaning back in his chair, with an ankle on the opposite knee, he looked relaxed, but Addi could tell he wasn't, not really. His green eyes were wary, and a muscle jumped in his rigid jaw. His shoulders were tight with tension, and he played with the laces of his shoes.

Addi tried to think of a response, and eventually settled on, 'Why would you think that us marrying would be a good idea? It's the twenty-first century, Jude, people don't get married because of babies any more.'

He nodded and rubbed the back of his neck, but didn't drop his eyes. 'I have reasons why I think it's a viable option.'

A viable option. *Good grief.* As a little girl and teenager, even as a young adult, she'd imagined a proposal that had the love of her life down on one knee, preferably holding a huge diamond ring that could be seen from space.

She'd grown up and realised that life didn't work that way, but she'd never thought both her marriage proposals would be so lacking in romance. Dean had suggested they marry over a bowl of popcorn while they'd watch an action movie, and two weeks later had tossed a ring box at her, telling her to let him know if it didn't fit. Now Jude's proposal—or was it a suggestion?—contained the words 'viable' and 'option'.

'Would you like to hear them?'

She might as well. And afterwards she'd say no, they could move on and, maybe, discuss something familiar, such as Thorpe's hospitality division.

'When I say married, I am talking of a marriage of convenience—it wouldn't last more than a year, maybe eighteen months. And nobody would need to know that.'

Well, wasn't this just sounding better and better?

Jude frowned and tipped his head back to look at the ceiling. When his eyes met hers again, he leaned forward and placed his forearms on the desk, looking deadly serious. 'Look, I know you are worried about your job with Thorpe, but if you marry me I'll pull you over into a position at Fisher International. Whether you accept my job offer or not, I will pay all your medical bills and hefty monthly maintenance, starting this month.'

She wished she could say that she would dismiss his offer, that it wasn't attractive, but to someone who had mastered the art of stretching her budget it was. How could it not be? 'Go on.'

'I will also pay the fees of the best family law practitioner in the country so that you can keep your sisters with you.'

That alone was a huge incentive to tie herself to this man for eighteen months. Addi placed her hand on her heart, scared it would jump right out of her rib cage. He was making a good case for marriage, for explaining what she would get out of it. But so far it was all very one-sided. And she didn't, for a moment, believe that Jude

Fisher would give up his single status just to help her out.

He might occasionally be nice, occasionally thoughtful, always hot and sexy. But he wasn't a saint, and he wouldn't sacrifice himself on the altar of matrimony unless there was something in it for him.

She switched legs, half-turned, draped her arm across the back of the chair and nailed him with a look that said 'don't you dare lie to me'.

'Well, you seem to have the answers to my problems,' she commented, sounding a great deal more casual than she felt. 'So, what's in it for you?'

Jude drained his coffee cup and considered her question. Now came the tricky bit. How did he explain to her that, business-wise, having an illegitimate child was the worst thing that could happen to him? How did he explain that he was still being punished for a youthful mistake, for messing up? How could he even start to explain that his errors of judgement had caused Bart to lose all faith in him, so much so that he'd rewritten his will just a day after the story of Jude being conned by Marina hit the headlines?

Fishers didn't air their dirty linen in public, it simply wasn't done, and it would always be Jude's fault for letting that happen. He now had a minor paranoia about his privacy, and the thought of the contents of his grandfather's will, the fact that all his decisions had to be approved by a board of trustees and that he'd have to marry to keep his company under his control, made him want to break out in hives.

This situation was fraught with peril, and he had to be very careful about what he said.

'I don't know if you know that I was raised by my grandfather—he died about nine years ago,' he began, tapping the end of his pen against the surface of the sleek, designer desk.

Sympathy flashed across her face. 'I think I remember reading something in the press,' she replied quietly. 'I'm so sorry, Jude. Was he your only family?'

'He was, from the time I was a young kid.' When he caught her wince, he thought he should explain. 'Briefly—my mum died unexpectedly and my father checked out in every way a father could. When he died, Bartholomew took me in, but he wasn't a warm and fuzzy guy. Honestly, he was more of a headmaster or a bank manager than a father figure.

'We weren't close, and Bartholomew had very definite ideas on how I should live my life and what was expected of me. Unfortunately for him, I didn't always live up to those expectations,' he continued.

Addi linked her hands around her knees, looking intrigued. 'Well, if it's any consolation, Joelle didn't have *any* expectations of us, except that we did not inconvenience her any more than what was strictly necessary.' She waved her words away. 'Sorry, this is about you, not me. How do your grandfather's wishes connect to us getting married?'

He drummed his fingers against the surface of the desk. 'My grandfather and I had a falling out when I was nineteen. I got caught up in something I shouldn't have and it damaged our relationship.' Jude pushed fingers into his right temple to push away his headache. 'Then another lack of judgement on my part led to that incident being revisited, and my grandfather's blood pressure went through the roof. He died about three months later but not before he'd made certain amendments to his will.'

He was grateful she didn't prod and pry. He'd never told anyone about Marina, how naive he'd been. Correction: he'd never told anyone since Jane had broken his confidence by spilling his story to a tabloid to exact revenge.

Addi's dark eyebrows shot up. 'I presume those amendments are why you want us to marry?'

She was so very smart and quick on the uptake. He liked the fact that she could keep up with him and that she could look at a situation with pragmatism.

'My grandfather would never leave his company, the company his own grandfather started, to anyone outside of the family. But he had major doubts about my suitability to run his empire. He had questions about my judgement.'

Addi leaned forward, a small frown appearing between her eyebrows. 'I don't understand why, because you're one of the most respected people in the industry. You've grown Fisher International, consolidated and increased your market share. You run a good company.'

He couldn't help feeling pleased, and a little proud, hearing her words. 'My lack of judgement was in my personal life, not my business life, but Bartholomew couldn't differentiate between the two.'

'Ah.' She leaned back and wrinkled her nose. 'So tell me what was in his will.'

He couldn't tell her that—not yet. No, not *ever*. No one knew, except for Thabo, Cole Thorpe, Bart's lawyer and the Council of Three. And the trustees wouldn't say anything because Bart had made them sign a non-disclosure agreement. To reinforce their silence, Jude also paid them a substantial yearly allowance. 'That's not pertinent to our discussion. What is relevant is that I cannot have an illegitimate child.'

Strangely, the desire to tell her more, to share his past, bubbled under his skin. There was a chance that Addi, with her unconventional mother, might just be the one person who would understand how difficult it was to have been raised by an unconventional parental figure, someone you were at complete odds with.

But he wouldn't tell her. He'd told Jane about Marina and look how that had turned out. But he'd never told Jane how sick, sad and miserable he'd felt after he'd finally accepted the truth about Marina. How he'd felt like an idiot for being conned, a fool for still loving her, weeks and months after kicking her out of his life. How he'd felt the burn of humiliation, the acidity of stupidity. Jane had reopened those wounds when she'd blabbed his story to the tabloids and they'd never quite closed again. He hated the press, but he hated the fact that he'd been so naive to trust Marina with his heart, and even more stupid to trust Jane with his past.

The caveats in his grandfather's will, the implication that he couldn't be trusted to make good decisions, was acid in an open-to-the-bone wound.

'You're not giving me very much to work with here, Fisher,' Addi complained.

He met her eyes and shrugged. 'Is it necessary for you to know my reasoning? I don't think so.

I'm offering you a very good deal, Addi. Financial security, money to pay the best lawyers to keep custody of your sisters, a job if you want it. All I'm asking for is a short-term, completely secret, marriage.'

She narrowed her eyes. 'Why does it need to be kept secret?'

Ah, he'd wondered when she'd ask that. 'If the press hears about it, they'll wonder about the length of our relationship, why we didn't have a big wedding; there would be a lot of interest.'

There would be references to Marina and his idiocy and they would openly speculate about whether he was making another mistake. And he didn't trust that one intrepid journalist wouldn't dig a little deeper and somehow, somewhere, find a copy of the trust document that implemented his grandfather's wishes. He didn't want the world, his colleagues and employees to see how little Bart had trusted and respected his heir. It wasn't likely to happen, but he couldn't take that chance.

Making headlines was a nightmare, having his past replayed was a night terror and having the contents of the trust revealed—it was confidential, but he didn't trust anyone—would be the worst indignity and seventh-circle-of-hell stuff.

No, it was better to keep it secret.

'What will happen if you *do* have an illegitimate child?' Addi asked.

He pulled a face. 'My business, and my reputation, would be seriously compromised.' And the Council of Three would stay on for another ten years and they would hamper his plans to expand Fisher International. And his frustration levels would hit the roof. He was so close, just a year away from complete freedom, and he would do anything—well, nearly anything—to have his financial and business freedom.

Even marry.

Addi picked up on his reluctance and didn't push, instead choosing to stand up and walk over to the floor-to-ceiling window, looking out onto the grey, cold ocean and the yachts in the harbour.

'What if I left your name off the birth certificate?'

That was an option but not a good one. He was a Fisher, his child would be a Fisher, and keeping his or her name off the birth certificate would be denying the child knowledge of where it came from. No, marriage was the best option for them both.

'Look, I didn't think I was going to have the opportunity to be a father—that normally comes with a relationship with someone—but, now that it's going to be a reality, I want my child to have my name, Addison. I want to be a part of its life, to be a father.'

He'd never trust anyone again with his heart. After his grandfather, Marina and Jane, he'd never allow anyone to have any say over what he did and how he did it. He'd tried love but it hadn't taken. Why go back for more?

'I might not want a day-to-day wife, someone in my space, but I do want to protect my company, so I think that we can come to an arrangement.'

'An arrangement,' she murmured, her voice low and cool. He'd never met anyone who hid her feelings as well as Addi, who could take anything thrown at her and remain calm. It made him want to prick that bubble of self-assurance, to pull away her layers to see who she really was beneath that layer of calm. It felt as though the only time he'd got to the core of her was when they'd made love. Within a few seconds of kissing him, she'd started to melt, and he'd tasted heat, demand and more than a little wild.

'So how would this work?' she asked, placing a palm on the window, her eyes fixed on the horizon. He followed her gaze and, there in the distance, a container ship skimmed along the horizon, barely discernible in the mist and rain.

He saw a stab of longing in her eyes and wondered if she was wishing she could run away from her life and her responsibilities, from the daily grind. He had only himself to worry about and he did what he wanted, when he wanted, but Addi had responsibilities he hadn't. She juggled a family, a demanding job and handled the financial demands of a young family, mostly on her own. And, on top of what had to be a normally stressful life, she was worried about her job, was facing her sisters being taken from her and was pregnant.

How was she still standing?

And when had she last had a break, some time out? He suspected it was never. A holiday would be way down on her list of priorities, if it featured at all. It was obvious, even to a Neanderthal like him, that she could do with some down time.

'Still waiting, Jude.'

Right, she'd asked him how he thought their fake marriage would work. 'After the prenuptial agreement is signed, we marry quietly without fuss or fanfare. I'll take care of the paperwork.

'Once we marry—preferably as soon as possible—we carry on as normal, with you in your house, me in mine. You hire a law firm to fight for custody, I'll pay those costs and I'll guarantee you a job within the hospitality division of Fisher International, at a higher salary than you are getting now. I will also pay you maintenance and child support, starting immediately. Money will never be a problem for you again, Addison.' Her breath seemed to hitch, and Jude couldn't decide whether that was a sigh of relief or a hint that she was scared. Both, maybe?

'How long do you want us to stay married?' Addi asked him, turning around to look at him.

'At least six months after the birth of the baby, more if we can manage it.' By the end of the following year, he'd have the company, be rid of the trustees and would be free to do what he wanted.

She held his eyes for the longest time, hers bright-blue but dancing with fear, anxiety and more than a little hope. Having her money issue solved was a big deal but he knew that him funding the lawyer's fees for her upcoming custody battle meant more to her. She just wanted stability, a little room to breathe. He could give that to her and wouldn't break a sweat—the amount they were talking of was petty change to him. All he required was for her to be legally tied to him for a year, maybe eighteen months.

'What's the process?' she asked. 'What do we need to get married?'

'All I'll require from you is a signature on some documents and then I'll arrange for someone to marry us. I thought that as soon we are—' he hesitated and decided to choose different words. 'As soon as that's done, we could get back to business and start with the inspection of the Thorpe hotels. I'd like to start with the lodge in Mozambique…uh… Something Bay?'

He wasn't sure how he was going to cope with the object of all his sexual desires dressed in a bikini, but he'd cross that bridge when he came to it. All he knew for certain was that they should leave the country as soon as possible, and that in Mozambique he could arrange for her to have a little down time. She definitely needed it.

'Turtle Bay,' she corrected him. 'What about the prenup? How complicated is that going to be?'

He thought about his too-picky lawyer, who was going to have a thousand questions and who'd want to prepare for five thousand possible eventualities. By the time Kara was done, they'd have a fifty-page agreement that would take six years to read through and digest. This was a good arrangement for Addi; she was getting a lot out of this, and she wouldn't screw him over. It didn't mean he trusted her—he didn't trust a woman with anything more than ordering her own meal at a restaurant—but he did understand that she had a lot to lose by not agreeing to his terms.

Kara would scalp him for this…but that didn't stop Jude from digging out a legal pad from his desk drawer and writing his name, then Addison's, across the top of the page with the words 'Prenuptial agreement' below. Keeping it simple, he wrote a few paragraphs, detailing their agreement and his requirement for secrecy. His sentences didn't fill up more than half a page. He drew a line for them each to sign, scribbled his name and the date and handed her the paper to sign.

Addison lifted her eyebrows and shook her head. For a minute, he thought she'd crumple it up in her fist, but then she surprised him by shrugging, placing the paper on the edge of his desk and asking for his pen.

She signed her name in a neat script and handed the paper back to him. 'I'd like a copy of that, please,' she told him, her tone crisp. Then he caught the amusement in her eyes, and he grinned. They were going to do this. They were going to get hitched.

If someone had asked him a week ago to write a list of the top one hundred things he might be doing the following Monday, signing a handwritten pre-nup would not have featured on his list.

CHAPTER SIX

ADDI STOOD IN front of the robed priest in a tiny chapel, the midday sun illuminating the stained-glass window above the altar. She shuffled her feet and, feeling Jude's eyes on her, lifted her head to meet his eyes. He gave her a reassuring smile and turned his attention back to the tiny priest, who'd insisted on giving them a homily on marriage.

She'd been unsure of what to wear to her wedding that wasn't really a wedding, so she'd chosen to wear a navy coat-dress with sheer stockings and her highest black heels. She was glad she'd made an effort because Jude looked smart and sombre in his dark-grey suit, white shirt and mint-green tie.

She was about to be married—if she wasn't already, given the sheaf of documents she'd signed in the chapel's anteroom. Addi swallowed down a surge of panic. How had it come to this?

Addi felt Jude's hand surround hers and he

lifted it to tuck it under his arm. Thankful for the support, she shuffled closer to him and gripped the crook of his elbow, breathing deeply.

It would be okay…it *had* to be okay.

But, damn, she wouldn't have been human if she hadn't thought of how different her wedding day could've been. And she couldn't help comparing it to the excitement she'd felt preparing for her wedding with Dean, before the girls had dropped into her life.

She'd been so in love, looking forward to the future, ecstatic about sharing her life with a man whom she'd thought adored her. With Jude, it felt as if all her emotions were super-charged and she knew that, if this had been a proper wedding, something they'd both wanted and looked forward to, she would be the human equivalent of a Catherine wheel. Buzzing, spinning, glowing and glinting…

Would she ever experience that? Probably not. Devastation pierced her pragmatism and for a moment, a step out of time, she wanted it all. Standing there, her arm in his, Addi craved love, security and the stability of being loved by, and committed to, a strong, smart, decent man.

Someone like Jude.

Think about work, Addison. Think about anything else until you can face the thought that you are someone's—no, Jude's—wife. With more willpower than she'd thought she possessed, Addi forced herself to turn her thoughts from the priest's long-winded sermon to work and remembered that she'd received correspondence from Thorpe Industries, London, yesterday.

The memo had stated that Cole Thorpe was in the process of selling the assets he'd inherited from his brother and that, while he would issue severance packages, he suggested his staff consider other employment options.

That meant that Lex, who worked as a part-time driver for Thorpe, would need to look for alternative work. While she didn't bring in a lot of money, driving for the company did pay for her university modules and exam fees. As his driver, Lex had been spending a lot of time with Cole but, given the craziness of her life lately, Addi hadn't had much time to connect with her sister. She had asked what Lex thought about Cole but her normally garrulous sister had avoided the question. And blushed. Was something happening between the billionaire and her sister?

Maybe. Lex deserved to have some fun. Or maybe Lex was simply worried about her job. Addi wished she could reassure her and tell her that Jude was going to pay her maintenance and that she had a job waiting for her at Fisher International when it was time to move on from Thorpe.

But, if she explained that much, then she'd have to explain how it all came about. None of her explanations would make sense without telling Lex why she needed money so quickly and explaining her decision to marry Jude. She'd promised Jude their marriage would remain a secret and, because Joelle was the master of broken promises, she took any vows she made super-seriously.

She hated lying, even if it was by omission. But the simplest solution, the one that would allow her to keep her vow to Jude, would be to wait until she started at Fisher International, tell Lex she'd received a massive increase and that their money troubles were a thing of the past.

It was the truth, sort of. If she massaged it really, really hard.

Addi bit the inside of her cheek as she tried to convince herself that she was shutting her sister out for everyone's greater good. That Lex would understand that she was taking such a drastic step for her, Nixi and Snow.

Lex also had the right to know that Joelle was suing for custody, but if she told her Lex would lose it. She would start to worry, to fret, and her stress would affect the girls. Lex couldn't afford to be distracted right now; she had an exam coming up, exams she couldn't afford to fail. No, she'd tell Lex after she got some feedback from the family lawyers she'd hired yesterday, when she knew what were their chances of keeping custody of Nixi and Snow. Hopefully, this custody battle would be all a storm in a teacup, and she could avoid worrying Lex at all.

Addi wanted to spare Lex any worry she could. She also wanted to tell her about the baby, but she was embarrassed to have made such a mistake when she was supposed to be so supersmart. She felt as if she'd let Lex down, and that she wasn't providing a good example to her sisters by doing what their mother had done... five times! How did she tell them to be careful, to take precautions, to be sensible, when she'd messed up so badly? She felt like an utter fool.

She knew what she *should* do but she wasn't ready to tell Lex, she wasn't ready to tell *anyone*, her life-changing news. She was still wrapping her head around the events of the past days, coming to terms with everything that had happened. When she felt stronger, when she was in a stronger position mentally and financially, she'd tell her sisters she was pregnant, that they were financially secure and that everything would be fine.

She'd leave out that she was married. Besides, this wasn't a proper wedding anyway. If it had been, she'd have had Lex as her maid of honour, Storm as her bridesmaid and Nixi and Snow as flower girls. She would have worn a white dress with a veil, and she would have fizzed with happiness instead of carrying around a heavy boulder in her stomach. Jude would have looked at her with love in his eyes instead of wariness and, after they exchanged rings, they'd have shared their first kiss as man and wife.

Yes, it was sad that her first wedding, probably her only wedding, wasn't the fairy-tale day Addi had expected and dreamed of, but this was real life, and, as Lex would say, she had to suck it up. Real life demanded practicality and pragmatism: happy-ever-afters were a myth, and love and commitment frequently ran when adversity knocked on the door.

This was a business arrangement, a legal arrangement. Despite them being in a chapel, nobody could call this a wedding ceremony.

Business. Arrangement.

And, since that was *all* it was, she could hold off telling Lex. But, man, she still felt guilty.

The priest cleared his throat and Jude covered his hand with hers, his gentle squeeze bringing her out of her thoughts. 'I understand there are no rings to be exchanged?' the priest asked, managing to look disapproving.

'Unfortunately, they are getting resized and

weren't ready in time,' Jude replied, his lie sliding smoothly off his lips. They couldn't wear rings, of course, because no one could know they were married.

The priest sniffed his disapproval. It was obvious that he thought that something was off but, judging by the faded furniture and the cracks in the walls, Jude had chosen this church so that he could make an enormous donation in exchange for the priest's silence.

Addi couldn't judge him; she was getting married because she needed Jude's money too.

The priest looked at Jude. 'Do you promise to love, honour, cherish and protect her, forsaking all others and holding only unto her for evermore?'

Addi gulped. Those were terribly serious, portentous words.

Jude didn't hesitate. 'I do.'

My turn.

Addi forced down a hysterical giggle. This couldn't possibly be her life. Addi Fields, control freak, didn't enter marriages of convenience.

'Do you promise to love, honour, cherish and protect him, forsaking all others and holding only unto him for evermore?'

Um...uh...

Could she do this? Should she do this? Addi didn't know if she could say the words and commit herself to this extraordinary course of action. But then she recalled the photograph hanging in the hallway of her home. It was a candid shot of the five sisters, arms around each other, laughing.

Yes, she could do this. She *would* do this. It was her job to look after them, to protect and nurture them, and this was the only solution available to her.

Addi lifted her chin and looked from the priest to Jude and back again. 'I do,' she said, her voice strong and clear.

'By the power vested in me, I now pronounce you man and wife.'

Well, there was definitely no going back now.

Addi stepped inside the *casinha*, a 'small house' down the beach from the dining area of Turtle Bay, and looked around at the wood, thatch and canvas structure. A huge double bed was covered in white linen and a filmy mosquito net was wrapped around the makeshift tree-trunk four-poster bed. She knew, because it was her job to know, that there was a slipper bath and an open-air shower—also with amazing views.

Hers was the smaller of the two cabins, and Jude was occupying the much larger one next door. He had a larger deck and a hammock strung between two trees. Their front garden was the white beach and gorgeous sea, and their back garden was a wild coastal forest.

Addi kicked off her shoes and half-pulled her shirt out of her skirt, thinking the band in her pencil skirt was a bit tight. She'd started to put on a bit of weight, not surprisingly, since she was feeding and growing a little human.

Addi placed her hand on her stomach, the thought punching her in her gut. Up until now, and apart from her not being able to drink coffee, the baby had been more of an intellectual exercise, a thought rather than reality. But with her stomach expanding, and with her feeling very tired, she was starting to feel the physical changes.

'Are you okay?'

She jerked her head up and saw Jude standing on the deck of her cabin. He'd changed into a pair of swimming shorts and a loose, half-buttoned cotton shirt, sleeves haphazardly rolled up to reveal his tanned and muscular forearms.

'Fine,' Addi said, managing a quick smile. Last night he'd surprised her by whisking her from the church and treating her to an evening at Snell's, Cape Town's most exclusive restaurant. Thanks to knowing the owner, Patrick Snell, Jude had managed to snag an ultra-secluded table in the private dining room, the one with the best view of the city's waterfront. The food had been exceptional, the service flawless and he'd made an effort to put her at ease.

After their meal, he'd driven her back to her house in Green Point and left her with a kiss on the cheek and a soft smile. It had been an exceptionally weird, and ridiculously chaste, wedding night.

When she'd met Jude at the airport earlier, she'd been quickly reminded that theirs hadn't been a real wedding because Jude had treated her like a colleague and not the woman he'd married the day before. Despite Addi knowing that they were heading for a tropical island, Jude's business-like approach was the bump back to earth she'd desperately needed. This was a business deal, they hadn't made a lifelong commitment and, despite the white beaches and turquoise sea, this was most definitely *not* their honeymoon.

Until she'd seen the beach and the romantic cabin, she hadn't realised how much she wanted to step out of time and revel in being the sole focus of a sexy man's attention.

It was just one more thing that wasn't meant to be.

She gestured to her laptop bag. 'So, if you give me a moment to set up, we can get to work. I meant to do some work on the plane, but I couldn't keep my eyes open. Sorry about that.'

His lips firmed and she knew he was unhappy about her lack of professionalism. Despite the craziness of the past week, she would not let her standards slip.

Jude looked to the Indian Ocean, a lovely, sleepy blue, and looked at her. 'Addi, it's three-thirty in the afternoon. It's already been a long day and there is no way I am going to look at spreadsheets and figures now. And neither are you.'

That sounded like heaven. Addi rubbed her foot on the back of her calf. 'Jude, we need to work. This isn't a holiday, at least it's not for me.'

'Actually, it is,' Jude told her. He walked into the bedroom area, picked up her laptop bag and tucked it under his arm. 'I'm confiscating this.'

'You can't do that!' she cried, lunging for it, but because Jude was so much taller he simply lifted the bag up and out of her reach.

'Want to bet?' he grinned. Seeing her con-sternation, his smile faded. 'Addi, it's Thursday afternoon—we're staying here until Monday af-ternoon. It's been a long, rocky, tense ten days for both of us, for you more than me. You are mentally, physically and emotionally exhausted.'

Well, yes, maybe a little more than normal.

'For the next four days, you are not going to work, or even think about work. You're not going to do anything but eat, sleep and relax,' Jude added.

Oh, God, that sounded like heaven. Her eyes filled with tears at the thought of doing nothing. 'But—'

'Work will still be there on Monday afternoon,' Jude assured her, tucking her beloved laptop under his arm. 'And, because I don't trust you to not sneak in some hours, I'm going to take this.'

Addi bit her lip, tempted, but unsure whether this was a wise course of action. She could deal with terseness, with work demands and requests for figures and facts, but tenderness and thoughtfulness disarmed her. She genuinely had no idea how to deal with it and, worst of all, it made her realise what she'd missed out on.

She'd had so little kindness and thoughtfulness directed at her from men—Dean had been quite self-absorbed, her biological dad couldn't have been bothered and, while her ex-stepdad Tom had been great, his kids had come first and rightly so. She wasn't sure how to respond to Jude's kindness.

And, without work as a barrier between them, what would they talk about and how would they interact? Apart from that hot, wild night when they'd slept together, and the dinner they'd shared last night, she and Jude hadn't spent any quality time together. Last night they'd discussed the food and the hotels in Thorpe Industries' portfolio, nothing more personal than that.

And what about sex? If they took work away, would all those inconvenient wants and needs come rolling back in? Would they find each other hard to resist? Would they end up in bed again? This was a business arrangement, but she still had the hots for Jude, and frequently spent her nights reliving the way he'd touched her, trying to remember exactly how he tasted, the feel of his hot skin under her hands.

'I have never heard anyone who thinks as loudly as you do,' Jude complained.

Addi rocked from foot to foot and shrugged.

Jude leaned his shoulder into one of the tree trunks that served as a pillar of the four-poster bed. 'Are you worried that if we don't have work to fall back on, your precious figures and spreadsheets, we won't have anything to talk about? Are you concerned that our time together will be awkward? Or are you worried that we might lose our heads and fall into bed again?'

How did he read her mind? *How?*

Jude smiled at her shock. 'I'm not expecting you to entertain me and I'm very comfortable with silence,' he told her, reaching out to touch her hair. 'And, if we do end up in bed again, that's fine too.'

'We're working together. And we're married!' Addi told him, sounding and feeling flustered.

'Should I point out that married people often have sex?' His mouth quirked up at the corners before his expression turned serious when she didn't smile. 'If we end up sleeping together, Addi—and that will be your choice—it will be absolutely and utterly separate from work and our agreement, our marriage of convenience. It'll be because you want me and I want you.

'Clear?' he asked when she didn't reply.

She nodded, feeling as though he'd pulled all the wind out of her sails. She didn't have a comeback, didn't have an argument. Neither was she looking for one. All she wanted to do was to pull on her swimsuit and immerse herself in that luscious-looking sea, dig her bare toes into the warm sand and tip her face to the sun.

Jude sent her an understanding smile. 'Get changed, Addison, and let's hit the beach.'

Now, there was one order she was happy to obey.

After just one day of lying in the sun and bobbing in the waves, Addi looked as though she'd been here for a week, Jude decided. They sat at the intimate outdoor restaurant situated in the centre of the beach, the *casinhas* spread out to either side of the casual but luxurious dining and lounge area. Behind the tables was an open-air kitchen where the chef conjured up stunning meals that ranked up there with the best he'd eaten in his life.

Together with the luxury décor, the superbly kitted out *casinhas* and the amazing beverage section, he understood why this fifteen-bed resort commanded such high prices. The beach was why people came to Turtle Bay but there was more to do than just sun tanning and swimming. Earlier, he and Addi had taken a walk on a trail in the coastal forest behind them, and he could easily arrange to go on a game drive, as there was a private game reserve just a short drive away.

Tomorrow, they were taking a boat ride to snorkel over a reef far out to sea. He couldn't wait.

Jude picked up his beer and took a long sip, his eyes dancing between the lovely view in front of him—the sunset was a riot of pinks and purples—and the equally lovely woman beside him. Addi was a little flushed, her nose even pinker than her face, and she wasn't wearing any make-up. Her hair was more messy than usual, but in her acid-green bikini, a brightly coloured sarong knotted on her right hip, she looked stunning. A beautiful beach babe with bright hair and blue, blue eyes.

But beyond her looks was a woman who intrigued him, someone strong, capable and so damn brave. Whenever he looked at her, he experienced a strange jumble of emotions: lust and need, and behind those a need to protect and understand. He wanted to dig, to discover, something he didn't usually spend his energy on. Lust was normally enough but Addi made him feel as though he were standing in an emotional tornado, being battered from all sides.

He was also, strangely, very unsatisfied with how they'd got married. He'd chosen that out-of-the-way church because it would afford them maximum privacy but, standing in front of that gnome-like priest, he'd wanted more. For a moment—okay, a couple of moments—he'd let his imagination run away with him and he'd imagined Addi in a stunning dress, her face alight with joy, surrounded by their friends and family, eager to walk up the aisle to him. Excited about sharing a life with him...

Wow. What had happened to the self-reliant, independent, emotionally distant man he'd been before he'd met her? He'd like him back, please.

'This is such a stunning place,' Addi said, turning those magnificent eyes on his. Her chin rested in the palm of her hand and her lovely mouth curved up in delight. 'Thank you for giving me the time off.'

'You needed it,' Jude told her. He gestured to her empty glass. 'Would you like another lime and soda?'

She wrinkled her sunburned nose. 'What I would like is a mojito,' she told him. 'But I can't drink alcohol so, yep, another lime and soda would be great.'

Jude looked around and within a couple of seconds he'd placed her order. 'How many of the Thorpe properties have you visited?' he asked, curious.

She shook her head. 'Maybe two…both of them in the Western Cape. I've never stayed at a resort before.' She lifted her shoulder and her cheeks turned pink. 'This is only the second time I've stayed at a hotel.'

He frowned. 'But didn't you take holidays as a kid?'

'You're mistaking my mother for someone who'd consider spoiling us that way. And you're assuming we had money to go on holiday. She didn't and we didn't. Surviving was sometimes a challenge.'

'Tell me,' he said softly. He wanted to know her history, what made her tick, the forces that had shaped her. He knew he was playing with fire—he should be putting some distance between them—but he couldn't help wanting to know more. Everything. He was in so much trouble here.

She stared at the sunset and when the waiter, Miguel, arrived with her drink, she thanked him and lifted the straw to her mouth.

'Joelle had us young—she was just eighteen when she had me, nineteen when Lex was born. She dragged us from house to house, living with anyone—and by anyone, I mean a man—who'd give her free board and lodging.'

He didn't know how to ask but he had to. 'And were they...okay, these guys?'

Addi nodded and he swallowed his sigh of relief. 'One or two were dodgy but nothing happened.'

Despite his parents' death—his mum's had been particularly traumatic—he'd still lived a privileged life. He'd grown up in a mansion, attended the best boys' school in the country, had every toy and piece of branded clothing a kid could want and he'd enjoyed overseas beach, snow and cultural holidays. His school tours hadn't been to the local museum but to places like Russia and the Caribbean. He thought about telling her that he was spoiled and lucky, but figured she knew that already.

'Our best times were when Joelle met and married Tom, Storm's dad. That was our longest stretch of stability, about three years.'

He frowned, confused. 'Who is Storm again?'

'My middle sister. She's twenty-four, six years younger than me. Technically, you have four sisters-in-law,' she quipped. Then she grimaced. 'Sorry, maybe I shouldn't have said that.'

He smiled, wanting to put her at ease. 'Why not? It's temporarily true.'

'You should thank God this isn't Regency England and that you don't have to provide dowries for all of them.'

'In the African culture, I'd have to pay lobola to your sisters for allowing me to marry you,' Jude pointed out. 'Cattle are damn expensive.'

'I'm probably only worth about two chickens and a goat,' Addi quipped.

He laughed. 'If that.'

She nudged him with her shoulder, but he was happy to see she could take a joke. 'You mentioned an Aunt Kate before…tell me about her.'

'By the time we hit our teens, Joelle was finding it very difficult to persuade her lovers to let her, and her two stroppy teenagers, move in. We really bounced around for a few years; it was incredibly stressful. Then Joelle reconnected with her mum's sister; they'd fallen out years before. We went to stay with her for what was supposed to be a few weeks during the long summer holidays, and Joelle said that she was going out to look for a stable job. We didn't mind; Aunt Kate was old and strict, but we had three meals a day.'

Addi ran an elegant finger up and down her glass. 'Joelle didn't come back. When she finally showed up, two months later, Aunt Kate wouldn't let us leave. We stayed and have been in her house ever since.'

'And she paid for you to go to uni?'

Addi nodded. 'Well, her insurance policy did. After she died, we rented out rooms in the house to other students to help fund our living expenses and Lex picked up a job. The plan was for me to get my degree as quickly as I could, and then I'd help Lex pay for her to go to uni. But then Joelle dropped back into our lives, surprising us with two half-sisters we didn't know about.'

'She never told you about them?'

'Nope. She rocked up with them. She'd been living in Thailand. She asked us to take them for the weekend...'

He connected the dots immediately. 'And she did a runner.'

'We couldn't believe she'd suckered us like she did our aunt Kate. And, like Kate, we took them in. I mean, what else could we do?'

Jude tipped his beer bottle to his mouth. 'And she's still in Thailand, right?

'Mmm...'

'Why do you think she wants them back? Why now?' he asked. 'Do you think she's had a come-to-the-light, repent-of-her-sins moment?'

'Joelle?' Addi's eyebrows shot up. 'No way. No, I'm thinking that she's got a guy on the line, someone who is either very family oriented or someone who thinks that kids belong with their mum. Someone fairly rich, because she wouldn't be hiring a lawyer unless he was paying.'

Man, her mother sounded like a piece of work.

'Well, your lawyer will mop the floor with her lawyer,' Jude told her, covering her hand with his and squeezing it. As she'd told him earlier, she'd engaged a lawyer he'd recommended from a practice that had an excellent reputation in family law, and she'd forwarded all the correspondence from her mother's lawyers to hers. They'd acknowledged her email and asked for a retainer…

Damn, he'd forgotten to pay them, as per their agreement. This week hadn't only been difficult for Addi, but he was also slipping up. The hard part was over, he told himself, and they'd soon get used to their new set of circumstances. Within a week or two, they'd go back to normal. Whatever normal was.

Making a mental note to make the payment for the lawyers, Jude looked at Addi and fought the urge to take the fear out of her eyes and promise her that everything would be okay. From the moment he'd met her he hadn't been able to put her in a box, hadn't been able to stop himself from feeling more than he should. She'd burrowed under his skin, and he suspected that was where she'd stay. He desperately wanted to reassure her, promise her that everything would work out. The thing was, it frequently didn't. His mum's death from an undiagnosed ectopic pregnancy, his father's depression, Marina… Life had taught him that was a promise he couldn't make.

Some things, unfortunately, even money and power couldn't change.

Addi looked a little sick. 'I couldn't bear it if we lost them, Jude. I grew up with Joelle, and I know how unsettled life is with her, but they'd also be in a foreign country. Can you imagine how scary that would be for them? And Lex would be devastated. She's been their rock for the last four years. She adores them.'

He stroked her hair and ran his fingers over the bare, hot skin at the back of her neck. 'And you, Addi. How would you feel?'

'I'd miss them intensely and I'd feel gutted. And for the rest of my life I'd have to live with the fact that I failed those kids. That they looked to me to help them, and I couldn't, that I didn't.'

He pulled back from her and waited for her to look at him, for their eyes to connect. 'Addi, that's a big burden to place on your shoulders, a harsh way of looking at this. You took in those girls, you've paid for everything they need, have given them a bed and clothes and stability. You've loved them. And—and I'm pretty sure this won't happen—even if they do go back to their mum, you would've done everything possible to keep them here. How would that be a failure?'

Her eyes filled with tears. 'It just would be.'

He ran his knuckle down her cheek. 'You are very hard on yourself, sweetheart.' Because he was so close to kissing her, needing to chase her tears and sadness away with heat and passion, he leaned away from her and changed the subject. It was so easy to get sucked in by passion, to fall into the heat of the moment, and he had to keep his head. If he didn't, he'd end up dinged and dented again. Life with Addi was turning out to be a constant tug of war, between what he wanted and what he knew he couldn't have.

'How do your sisters feel about becoming an aunt?'

Embarrassment flashed in her eyes and she jerked back and folded her arms across her chest, looking a little belligerent. She didn't answer him and, when he cleared his throat, she lifted her eyebrows at him. 'What?'

'You haven't told them, have you?'

She pulled a face. 'No.'

'Why not?' he asked, interested. He thought she and Lex were close, that she would've told her everything—including that they'd had a one-night stand. He wondered if she knew that Lex and Cole were having a hot fling. It wasn't his place to tell her.

'Does she know that that we slept together? That we are married?'

'You asked me not to tell her about our marriage, and I promised I wouldn't, so I haven't,' she replied, sounding a little snippy. 'I didn't tell her about what happened at the Vane either.'

'Why not?' Jude didn't know why her answer was important, just that it was.

Addi took a large sip of her drink and he knew that she was trying to find a way to avoid answering. But when he kept his eyes on her face she sighed loudly. 'I wanted it to be just *my* memory…' She waved her hands in the air. 'I don't expect you to understand that.'

He did, actually. Those hours spent with her were some of the best of his life, and telling someone else, explaining, would dilute some of the magic.

'You're going to have to tell her about the baby at some point, Addi. I don't think that's something you can hide for ever.'

'I know, Jude!'

Addi lifted her thumb to her mouth and started biting at her cuticle, something he'd noticed she did when she was on edge. He pulled her thumb away and shook it gently. 'Spill it, Ads.'

She looked as though her gut was in a twist. 'I'm embarrassed to tell her!'

Okay, that wasn't what he'd expected. 'Why?'

'When we were sixteen, I sat Lex down and made her promise, swear on her life, that she wouldn't fall pregnant accidentally. I promised her the same. We vowed that having a baby would be a deliberate choice, made when the circumstances were right.' She made a sound that was a cross between a hiccup and a sob. 'It wasn't supposed to happen this way, Jude, especially given our history.'

He put his arm around her, grateful that his broad back hid her distress from the other guests who'd gathered in the restaurant bar. He rubbed his hand up and down her back, trying to give her what comfort he could. 'Your sister will understand, Addi.'

'I hope so,' she muttered, brushing her cheeks with the tips of her fingers. 'I don't want her to be disappointed in me, that's all.'

'I think you are being hard on yourself, Addi. We're allowed to make mistakes, to be human.'

Addi sniffed. 'God, how am I going to have the "you've got to be careful and use protection" speech with the girls when they are older? They'll laugh their socks off.'

'You'll tell them that mistakes happen and that, no matter what, you'll stand in their corner. That there's always a plan to be made.'

'Hopefully their plans won't be as drastic as ours,' she muttered.

'A perfect storm,' he agreed. If his grandfather hadn't been so damn unforgiving and so very controlling, his life and Addi's would be a lot easier. But there wasn't anything they could do about it. They were married. He had a wife. In a year, he'd have full control of his company.

A *temporary* wife, he corrected. In name only.

Addi pulled back from him and sent him a teary smile. 'Crazy set-up, huh?'

'Crazy.'

He looked into her eyes and saw the flash of interest, the heat burning in all that blue. She looked down at her hand, which lay on his forearm but, interestingly, she didn't break their connection.

'We had fun that night, didn't we?' she asked softly.

Fun? That was a tame word for the hottest, sexiest night of his life. He'd loved every second of their love-making and would love to do it again…and again.

He lifted her hand and placed an open-mouth

kiss on her palm, wanting and needing to gauge her reaction. Pink infused her cheeks. The tip of her tongue peeked out to lick her bottom lip and her eyes ducked to his mouth. Yeah, she wanted to be kissed. Hopefully wanted a lot more.

'I loved making love with you, Addison,' he told her, keeping his tone low. 'And I'd love to do it again.'

'For how long?' she asked.

'For now, let's say that for as long as we are out of the country, visiting Thorpe hotels,' he replied. 'Back home we'd have to be super-careful so that we don't grab any press attention.'

She frowned at that, then a cheeky smile pulled her lovely mouth upward. 'Well, on the plus side, at least I won't fall pregnant,' she quipped.

He smiled at her attempt at humour and then wondered if she was saying yes, if she was giving him the green light. Needing to know, he traced his thumb over her bottom lip. 'So, will you let me make love to you again, sweetheart?'

She stared at him and he held his breath. Eventually, what seemed like years later, she nodded. 'Yeah, I think I will.'

Not wanting to wait, or give her time to change her mind, and needing her, he stood up and tugged her to her feet. Addi looked from him to her half-empty drink to the still intensifying sunset. 'Now?' she demanded. 'Can we not eat something first?'

No. He wasn't going to wait—not for her. 'They have this amazing thing called room service,' he told her, wrapping his hand around hers and pulling her behind him as he weaved his way between the tables filled with amused guests. They knew exactly where they were heading but he didn't care.

This wasn't a honeymoon, but he was going to take any chance he could to have this wonderful, lovely woman naked. And what would be better than rolling around a big bed, with the sunset tossing reds and oranges onto her soft, smooth skin and the sea providing the background music?

CHAPTER SEVEN

JUDE LED HER across the sand and up onto his wooden deck. Addi caught a glimpse of a comfortable sitting area to the right, but he angled left and led her to the bedroom, which looked straight onto the sea and the setting sun. Stopping next to the bed, he held her face in his hands and looked down at her, his expression intense.

'Are you sure you want to do this, Addi?'

Yes, absolutely. She couldn't wait to undo the buttons of his shirt and spread the fabric apart, to run her hands across his wide chest, to lay her mouth on his hot skin. To kiss his mouth and get lost in his arms. She placed her hand on his shoulder and met his eyes, gazing at that intense shade of green she'd come to associate with passion and need and want. 'I want this, Jude. I want *you*.'

He lowered his head to kiss her, but she pulled back just a little. She just needed to check one little thing. 'This has nothing to do with our deal or my job or anything else, right?'

'This is only about the fact that I can't wait to kiss your lips, to run my hands down your naked body, to touch, taste and caress you. I've thought about little else for the last two months, trying to remember your smell, the softness of your hair, that sexy sound you make when you're turned on.'

He radiated sincerity, and she knew that, at this moment, they were a couple who simply wanted each other. This had nothing to do with the marriage certificate tucked into her bag or the agreement they'd made. Right now, he wasn't the rich billionaire, her sort-of boss, and she wasn't the mother of his unborn baby.

They were just a man and a woman who were extremely, maddeningly, attracted to each other.

'Addi, you're killing me here,' Jude muttered, his hand coming up to cover hers and squeezing. It was such a boost to her ego to have a man like Jude look at her as though she were all the Christmas presents he'd ever wanted.

She could no more resist him any more than she could stop time.

'Take me to bed, Jude,' Addi told him, her voice strong and sure. She craved him and needed to experience the orgasms that only he'd managed to pull effortlessly from her.

As soon as the words were out of her mouth, Jude covered her mouth with his, not hesitating to slide his tongue between her teeth to tangle with hers. He bent his knees just a little, and boosted her up his body, and Addi wrapped her legs around his hips, her core settling on the hard ridge of his erection.

Yes, please.

This was exactly where she wanted to be.

Jude kissed her deeply and voraciously, demanding she meet his pace, and she was happy to. She tugged his shirt up his back to glide her hands over the bare skin of his back, loving the taut muscles and his harnessed strength. He held her so easily, with one arm beneath her butt, while his other hand covered her breast. He ducked his head to pull her nipple into his mouth, enjoying the friction created by her bikini top on her hard nipple. But that wasn't enough for Jude, and he tugged the strings holding the triangles together and pulled her bikini top from her body.

Allowing her to slide to her feet, he put one hand behind his head to grip the collar of his shirt and pulled it over his head in that sexy move only men managed to pull off. Addi reached forward to place her open mouth on his muscled chest but, before she could, he tugged off her sarong, leaving her to stand in just a pair of brief bikini-bottoms.

Jude pushed her bikini bottoms down her hips and her clothes lay in a colourful heap on the floor. He batted her hands away and made short work of removing his swimming shorts. She couldn't help herself, she needed to touch him, so she ran the side of her thumb up his shaft, unable to believe that a man could be so soft but so hard at the same time. She loved touching him, and wanted to inhale him, taste him, hear him moan her name as he struggled to control his reaction to her...

'If you keep looking at me like that, I'm going to lose it, sweetheart,' Jude warned her, his hand covering her breasts and his thumb dragging over her hard nipples.

Addi arched her back as she looked up at him. 'How am I looking at you?' she asked.

'Like I am a cupcake and you haven't eaten for days.'

Accurate.

Jude placed both his hands on her hips, lifted her and gently tossed her onto the enormous bed behind them. For a moment he stood next to the bed and looked at her, her legs slightly spread. She resisted the urge to place her hand on her mound, to cover her breasts with her arm. It was obvious that Jude very much liked what he saw and there was no reason to feel ashamed of being naked.

Jude placed his hands on either side of her head. Her eyes met his and she was unable to look away. He'd barely touched her, but she could feel his mouth on her breasts, his lips on her hip bone, between her legs.

As he started to turn the images in her head into reality, she wondered what it was about him that made her feel this way, why he was the only one who could make her feel out of control and how he could make her always active brain shut down. When he kissed or touched her she was able to disassociate herself from her life. She moaned as he switched his attention to her other breast, gently sucking her nipple so that it touched the roof of his mouth. He, and the way he made her feel, was all that was important.

Addi rested her weight on her elbows as she watched Jude's progress down her body, loving the way his lips skimmed across her rib cage and how he dipped his tongue into her belly button. He gently nipped at her hipbone with his teeth and that tiny hint of pain ratcheted up her pleasure, lifting her to another level.

If he didn't touch her soon she'd lose her mind—she desperately needed him to focus on her feminine secret places, where pleasures started and ended.

But Jude continued to tease her, kissing the inside of her thigh, inspecting a scar on her knee, running his tongue down her shin bone and sucking the soft spot on the inside of her ankle.

He'd done nothing more than kiss her, and stroke his long fingers over her super-sensitive skin, but she felt as though she was a bubbling cauldron about to overflow. But, as much as she wished to let loose, she wanted to give him some of the pleasure he'd given her, make him yearn, squirm and hopefully burn.

Wiggling away from him, she pushed his shoulders to get him to lie down and, when he rested on his back, she kneeled beside him, just taking her time to look, to pull in the details. His nipples were flat discs and the layer of hair on his chest was just enough to be sexy. It veered down into a thin trail across his hard, muscled stomach, and she traced the tan line across his lower stomach. His skin had tanned easily, turning the deep brown of surfers and sailors. He had the long legs of a runner and big, but surprisingly elegant, feet.

She ran her finger from the back of his broad hand and traced an upraised vein, stopping to inspect a scar just below his elbow. He lifted his other hand to put his hand behind his head, his biceps bunching, comfortable in his nudity. He had another scar just below his collarbone, the thin line suggesting he'd had surgery. She wanted to know what had happened and when, desperate to know everything about this man.

That was foolish, she thought as she dropped her head to place a kiss on his sternum, to drag her tongue down. They had a deal and, while they might be off-the-charts attracted to each other, they couldn't go tiptoeing around in each other's psyches. They had to keep their thoughts—and especially their feelings—out of this deal. If they didn't—and by 'they' she meant herself—life would become very complicated indeed.

Business deal, with some fun thrown in on the side.

No harm, no foul.

Taking her cue from him, Addi nipped his hipbone with her teeth and an instant later found herself on her back with Jude looming over her, his knee nudging her legs apart.

'I need you, Addison. *Now.*'

His voice was growly with need and desire, and Addi nodded, sighing when his erection probed her entrance. Instead of pushing inside her, Jude pushed his hand between her legs, and she released a low groan when his thumb brushed her bundle of nerves. He dragged his fingers through her warmth and wetness and his eyes glinted when they met hers.

'You're so damn sexy, sweetheart.'

She didn't need words, she needed him inside her, so she lifted her hips and pushed, sighing when he entered her. But it wasn't enough; she needed him inside her, as deep as he could go. Touching her soul, if possible.

'You feel like heaven,' Jude muttered as he rocked into her. 'Hook your legs around me.'

She obeyed his rough command and he slid a hand up her lower back, angling her up, and moved further inside her, as deep as he could go. This was what she needed, what she'd dreamed what sex should be.

Heat, passion, an intense build-up, rocketing hard and fast and detonating when she hit the edge of space, exploding into colour and sensation, into shards of nothing and everything.

Addi dug her nails into Jude's backside, dimly aware of his harsh breathing, his tensed body. She felt his release deep inside her and thought that making love with him without a condom felt more intimate, more intense. As she gathered her thoughts and her shattered pieces back together, she ran her hands up and down his broad back, over his firm buttocks. She loved his body. Loved the way he made her feel.

And she was terrified that, if she wasn't very,

very careful—if she didn't keep a sharp eye on her rebellious emotions—she could love him.

That would be a disaster of magnificent proportions.

Jude looked at Addi lying face-down in his bed, fast asleep. She had a white line across the middle of her back from her bikini strings, and he winced at her otherwise red skin.

He hadn't thought of her sunburn when he'd taken her, hadn't thought that the linen might aggravate her tender skin. Hell, he hadn't thought at *all*. He'd just wanted her and, as soon as she'd given him the green light, nothing but being inside her had entered his head. She'd chased every thought but being inside her out of his head.

She was so slim, Jude thought; nobody would think she was pregnant. Maybe she was one of those women who wouldn't look pregnant until she was way down the process, the ones who looked like they carried little balls under their shirts. He didn't mind what she looked like when she was pregnant—tiny or big and bold—as long as she and the baby came through the experience healthy.

He ran his finger down her spine, feeling each bump and admiring the delicious curve of her butt. He could stare at her for hours but, unfortunately, his rumbling stomach was demanding food. The moon was up and he lifted his left hand to look at his watch—it was nearly eight. If he wanted sustenance, he'd better order food soon.

Rolling off the bed, he pulled down the mosquito net and left Addi to sleep. Pulling on his swimming shorts, and a T-shirt, he decided to amble to the dining room, place an order and take a quick swim while he waited for their food to be delivered. Moving a screen in place so that the waiting staff wouldn't see Addi if they arrived at the cabin while he was swimming, he hit the beach, the light of the moon guiding his way.

He'd ordered line-caught fish for them both—he vaguely remembered something about pregnant women needing to avoid shellfish—and, after thanking Miguel, started the walk back to the *casinha*. He pulled off his T-shirt and ran into the sea, ducking under an incoming wave.

Jude bobbed in the waves, enjoying the moonlight dancing on the sea. The water was stunningly warm and it was a perfect night, with a slight breeze settling on his skin. He'd just had amazing sex, and was about to have a wonderful meal, but there was a little part of him that worried that this had all been too easy, that something was bound to go wrong.

At his next meeting with the Council of Three, he'd inform them of his marriage, that Addi was pregnant and assure them that the baby would be born legitimate. He'd remind them that his personal life fell under the NDA and that he'd sue if news of his marriage reached the papers. But, because he believed in sticks *and* carrots, he'd also send them an additional, unexpected, bonus.

He wasn't worried about the trustees ratting him out to the papers—money was an excellent motivator and he had lots of it. Unless a reporter got suspicious and went looking, they wouldn't unearth their quickie marriage, and Addi and him could quietly divorce after the baby was born.

But, because he considered all angles, good and bad, he considered the question of what he would do if the press found out that he was married. While he did not doubt that Addi would *try to* keep their wedding secret from her sisters, she might slip up and, if it got out, what then? He stared up at the moon, thinking about how he'd deal with that scenario.

They'd have to pretend that they were in love, and that getting married had been an impromptu decision. That they'd wanted to be married and take their time planning their church ceremony and the big reception everyone expected from one of the most eligible bachelors in the country. With some luck and some charm, nobody would ever find out that they'd married to get rid of his board of trustees. It would all be fine.

Nothing could go wrong.

Could it?

The next morning, Jude helped Addi climb down from the diving boat. They'd encountered wild dolphins and seen a manta ray and a huge turtle while they'd been snorkelling but, instead of seeing the same joy on her face as he did on the other guests', Addi's face looked a little pinched. He gathered her close and bent his head to speak in her ear. 'Are you okay?' he asked.

She nodded, tipping her head back to look at him. 'I think so.'

That wasn't a yes. He stepped back to look at her, glad to see that everyone else was walking up the beach and away from the speedboat. 'What's wrong?' he demanded.

Addi wrinkled her nose and placed her hand low on her abdomen. 'I've just got a little pain. It's not something I've had before.'

Every hair on his arms lifted as his skin cooled. Thoughts of what had happened to his mum battered him. 'How bad is the pain? Are you cramping?'

She looked at him as though he was losing his mind. 'It's just a dull pain, Jude. It's nothing.'

'How do you know it's nothing? Maybe there's

something wrong,' he said, admittedly sounding a little unhinged.

Addi sent him an 'are you mad?' look. 'Will you please relax? Geez, it's nothing serious.'

'How do you know?' he demanded, slapping his hands on his hips. 'You've never been pregnant before.'

Addi rolled her eyes so hard that he was sure she'd give herself a headache. 'I'm *fine*, Fisher.'

'When are you going to see a doctor? Have you made an appointment to get a scan?' He planted his feet in the sand as Addi wrapped her sarong around her hips. 'Maybe I should call my pilot up and get him to arrange for the Cessna to pick us up so that we can fly to Maputo.' He looked at his watch. It was eleven now; if they could leave by twelve, they could be in Maputo by half-one, meet his private jet and be in Johannesburg by three. His assistant would find a gynaecologist who could see her shortly after she landed. By the end of the day, she'd be getting treatment.

But, if she miscarried, where would that leave them? Divorced, he supposed. And the thought left him with such a bitter taste in his mouth that he felt slightly sick. He couldn't imagine her not being married to him, not carrying his child. But neither could he imagine a committed, day-to-day situation, living life with her. Or maybe he didn't want to imagine it because it scared him to the souls of his feet. If he lost his ability to be completely self-reliant, how would he scrape himself off the floor when it all went pear-shaped? And, nine out of ten times, it went pear-shaped.

Addi placed a hand on his bare chest and stared up at him, confused and a little irritated. 'Will you please calm down? I said that I'm a bit sore, not that there is anything wrong.'

'But don't you think we should get it checked out?'

Addi shook her head, her bright hair glinting in the sunlight. 'The pain is receding, it's almost gone. I think we should grab a drink, and you should take a breath. Or five.'

'Are you suggesting that I'm overreacting?'

She shook her head, her mouth curving up in a smile. 'No, I'm *telling* you you are overreacting. Just relax, Fisher. I'm not the first woman to fall pregnant, and I'm perfectly healthy.'

She was right, she wasn't the first, but what if the boat ride had been too bumpy, if she'd overdone it this morning? She was under his care and protection, and he didn't know enough about pregnancy to know what could cause a miscarriage or not. And, yeah, maybe there was a bit of fear that what had happened to his mum would happen to her.

Scrap that, maybe there was a *lot* of fear…

CHAPTER EIGHT

An hour later, they sat in the corner of the restaurant at their favourite table, one that was slightly isolated from the rest of the dining area. Jude had an icy beer in front of him and Addi wished she could order one herself; there was nothing better than a cold beer or cider after a morning spent on the beach or in the sea.

She'd had an amazing morning, one that she'd remember for the rest of her life. She, Jude and another couple had hopped aboard the dive boat and, within minutes, they'd been speeding north, the boat following the line of the coast. After ten miles, they'd came across a pod of dolphins which had been just as interested in them.

Within minutes, she'd pulled on a snorkel and dived off the boat, going as deep as she could and hoping that the dolphins wouldn't bolt at the sight of these strange white blobs in the water with them. As she'd come up for air, one dolphin had positioned itself next to her and mirrored her

vertical ascent, its stunningly intelligent eyes
on her face. When she'd broken the surface and
laughed, she'd seen it streaking away, and she'd
felt a surge of disappointment.

Ducking back under the surface of the mirror-
flat sea, she'd seen her new friend turn and speed
back toward her, circling her. She'd wanted to
reach out and touch the dolphin but figured that,
since she wasn't a fan of strangers touching her,
she'd give the mammal the same courtesy and
keep her hands to herself. She'd dived down, the
dolphin had followed, she'd come up and it had
mimicked her actions. As a test, Addi had spun
around in the water and had nearly gulped water
when the dolphin did the same.

When the dolphin had swum next to her and
nudged her stomach with its nose, Addi had
sensed that the creature knew she was carrying
a baby, another cog in the wheel of life. It had
been a deeply profound, amazing and emotional
experience and, when the dolphins had finally
left them, her dolphin being the last to leave,
she'd blamed her red eyes on the salt water, her
tears now part of the ocean.

They'd climbed back into the boat. The skip-
per and other guests had wanted to discuss the
experience to death, but Addi had been desperate for quiet, for some time to take in the almost
spiritual experience. Then Jude had gripped her

chin, placed a tender kiss on her lips and rested his forehead against hers, and she'd known he understood.

Some things didn't need discussion, and knowing that he didn't need explanations made her feel warm, a little gooey and, scarily, hopeful.

Be careful, Addison.

Addi took a long sip of lime and soda and looked out onto the bright-blue and green ocean. They would be leaving tomorrow, heading for Tanzania and another Thorpe hotel, but she didn't want to leave this spot and had no interest in returning to work. She wanted to stay here, in Jude's bed and arms, enjoying the trifecta of sun, sea and sex.

For the rest of her life, these few days would be the measure she judged her other holidays by. She'd also measure any other relationship she had in the future with the way Jude, her temporary fling, made her feel—wanted, sexy and seen.

The waiter deposited a plate of fried fish and salad in front of her, and a lobster roll in front of Jude, and she snagged a perfectly fried chip off his plate. She bit down and sighed. 'Those are absolutely divine.'

'Order yourself a plate,' Jude suggested.

She would have but she didn't want to turn

into a blimp. Joelle had remained reed-thin during her pregnancy with Storm—Addi's only memories of Joelle being pregnant—but that didn't mean she would too.

'Have you had any morning sickness?' Jude asked her, before lifting his beer bottle to his mouth.

'Nope. Except for my reaction to coffee, I've been fine,' Addi replied. 'It might still kick in but I'm hoping it won't. Throwing up isn't my idea of fun.'

She forked up some lettuce and a chunk of fish, and chewed. After swallowing, she decided to ask him about his over-the-top and uncharacteristically panicky reaction when she'd climbed off the boat. 'Why did you go into a meltdown when I said I had pain in my stomach?' she asked.

'I think calling my concern a meltdown is exaggerating,' Jude told her as he tucked into his lobster roll.

She nudged him with her elbow. 'You were all "let me call a plane", "let's get you to a doctor",' she told him. 'Are you normally such a worrywart?'

When he kept his eyes on his plate, and when his jaw tensed, she realised she'd hit a very big button. She didn't know how or why, but she intended to find out.

'What happened, Jude?' she quietly asked, and put her hand on his, squeezing gently.

He shrugged and took a bite of his roll, but Addi knew he wasn't tasting any of its delicate flavours. He could pretend to be insouciant, but she saw the pain in his flat green eyes and tension in every muscle in his body.

'You are, possibly, the most level-headed person I've met, so your reaction tells me that something very personal, and painful, happened to you. I'd love it if you shared that with me.'

He might or might not, but she could only ask. She could play the 'we're going to be parents' card, but she didn't want to force him to tell her, not that she really thought she could. She wanted him to tell her because he liked her, because he felt close to her, and because she thought they were friends as well as lovers.

When Jude finally spoke, his voice was pitched just loud enough for her to make out his words. 'My mum died from an undiagnosed ectopic pregnancy when I was eight. I was young when it happened, but I clearly remember her complaining of stomach pains. I suppose that memory kicked in when you said you were sore, and my brain jumped to the worst-case scenario.'

Understandable. 'Is me having a miscarriage something that worries you?' Addi asked him.

He lifted one big shoulder. 'To be honest, it's

been such a crazy time that I haven't given it that much thought. Or allowed myself to think about it.' He looked out to sea, his expression troubled. 'But maybe we shouldn't have married so quickly. There are sound reasons why most couples wait to announce that they are pregnant. It's because they don't want to get anyone's hopes up until the chance of miscarriage has passed.'

'If that happened, I wouldn't hold you to anything, Jude,' she assured him. 'I'm perfectly fine, and so is our baby.'

'How do you know?'

She had no idea. 'I just do.'

When Jude didn't respond, she thought it best that they move on to another subject. 'Tell me about your parents,' she suggested.

He took some time to reply. 'After my mum died, my dad withered away emotionally. Three years later, he was diagnosed with cancer. He tried chemo and radiation, but nothing took. He died about a year after being diagnosed. I think he died because he didn't want to live without her, and I wasn't enough.'

Addi felt her throat close, tears lodging there. 'I'm so sorry, Jude.'

'Love can be a pretty destructive force,' he told her. 'He only loved her; there was none left over for me.'

Oh, that was just awful, and he'd been so young. 'Who raised you?'

'My grandfather. He was an austere, introverted man who had no idea how to handle a lost, grieving boy with too much energy.' Jude drained his bottle of beer and signalled for another.

'I was sent away to boarding school when I was thirteen and didn't see much of him. I spent most of my school holidays at friends' houses. But I did get monthly letters from my grandfather, which I called "the Sermons". They were a detailed road map of what was expected of me as a Fisher. Essentially, he plotted and planned my entire life—he selected my degree, when I would join the family business, what university I would attend and how I would conduct myself. Basically, no wine, woman or song.'

She couldn't see Jude spending his university years as a studious monk and told him so. He smiled. 'The first year I went wild, I partied long and hard and had far too many one-night stands with women I barely remember. Grandfather, who kept tabs on me, was horrified. By the time Marina came along, he and I were barely speaking, and he was threatening to cut off my funding unless I returned to the straight and narrow.'

Marina? Who was she?

Jude thanked the waiter for his beer and

picked off half the label before answering her unvoiced question. 'She was this girl I met in a pub one night. Funny, gorgeous, intelligent. I fell—hard.'

She heard his voice crack and knew that, whoever this Marina person was, she'd hurt Jude badly. 'How long were you together?' Addi asked, trying to sound casual. She knew that if she threw a barrage of questions his way he'd shut down.

'Nine months, maybe a little more,' Jude replied. 'I was so in love with her. I thought she loved me, but I was very, very wrong about that.'

This hadn't been an ordinary youthful breakup, Addi realised. This hadn't been a burn bright, fade quickly situation. No, something had happened that had caused scars on Jude's psyche. Whatever had happened back then was still affecting the way he lived his life today. 'Will you tell me, Jude?'

'It's a long, ugly story.'

She'd grown up with Joelle—ugly didn't scare her. 'Tell me anyway.'

'My grandfather was already unhappy with me, furious that I'd spent my first year partying and that I'd barely scraped through. He didn't like my friends, the way I dressed, my lack of seriousness.'

'Did he keep that close an eye on you?'

'He did,' Jude confirmed. 'I'm not sure whether he hired a private investigator, or paid my friends for information, but he knew what I was up to all the time.'

Addi grimaced. Jude must've felt so betrayed by his grandfather's lack of trust. 'I started pulling back from my friend group,' Jude admitted. 'I didn't know who was feeding him information, so I cut everyone off. It was…hard.'

Of course it had been; at that age, friends were the lifeblood.

'In hindsight, I was the perfect mark for someone like Marina: a lonely, rich kid.

'I fell for her—hard,' Jude admitted. 'And we got serious fast. I saw myself being with her for ever. I thought that we'd finish our degrees, become independent and be stunningly successful together.'

'But?'

'But, as my grandfather took great pleasure in telling me, Marina tried to blackmail him. She said she'd break up with me and drop out of my life if he paid her off. If he didn't, she'd tell everyone she was pregnant and that I wouldn't let her leave. What she didn't realise is that old Bartholomew would've rather cut off his hand than give into extortion. He, via private investigators he'd hired, started digging into her life. It turned out that I wasn't the first, or the fifth, guy she'd pulled this stunt on. She was older—twenty-five—and mooching off rich boys was what she did.

'I didn't believe him, I believed her. I cut off ties with grandfather and refused to have anything to do with him,' he continued.

Addi saw the pain and anger in his eyes and knew there was more. 'Carry on, Jude.'

'I wasn't hopeful that Bartholomew and I would mend fences, so I picked up a job as a bar tender. I was working and studying and trying to keep it all together, to look after her and myself. I came home after a shift and she had a pill in her hand. She calmly told me that I either had to get my grandfather to pay up or she'd abort the baby she was carrying. It was the first I'd heard mention of a baby.'

Addi's mouth dropped open. 'She was *pregnant*?'

'That's what she said,' Jude muttered, bold and bright fury in his eyes. 'I looked at her and knew, just knew, that she wasn't. I knew she was lying, and I'd had enough. I was done being played. I tossed her, and her imaginary baby, out.'

Addi wrinkled her nose. 'And you are *sure* she wasn't pregnant?'

He sent her a *'really?'* look. 'She admitted it and told me playing the pregnancy card was worth a shot. Also, I saw her about five months later and she was as skinny as a rake. Nope, she wanted money and was prepared to do, or say, anything to get it.'

Addi wanted to go back in time and slap the woman. How dared she have played with Jude's emotions like that? And why was she feeling protective over this man? She only did that with people she loved…

She did *not* love him. That was too much, too soon…

You're overreacting, Addi. Rein it in.

'I'm sorry you went through that,' she told him. She pushed her half-eaten plate of salad away and reached for her drink. 'I know what being so disappointed by someone you love to distraction feels like.'

His head snapped up. 'Your mum?'

'Well, her too. No, I was engaged to a guy I met at university. I was due to marry him three months after the girls dropped into our lives. He decided they were more baggage than he could handle and he broke it off.'

She looked away and shook her head. 'That's not completely fair. He didn't sign up for a ready-made family and he did try, sort of, but they frustrated him. He *"tried"* for about three weeks—he kept telling me he'd do better—but then decided he couldn't.'

'I'm sorry,' he said, resting his forearms on

the table and shaking his head. 'It's a never-ending source of amazement to me that we are constantly bombarded with the news of relationships breaking up—this person had an affair, and that person wants out. Two out of three marriages end in divorce but, like lemmings, humans still keep stepping into the quagmire of marriage and are surprised when it doesn't work out. I don't get it.'

His words reminded her of a literary quote. 'Didn't Oscar Wilde say something about marriage being a dull meal with dessert served at the beginning?' She pulled a face. 'This is a pretty cynical conversation for two people who've just tied the knot.'

The corners of his mouth lifted in a smile. 'Ah, but the difference with us is that we have clearly defined expectations of what we want to achieve from our union and a time frame. A fling, with an option to carry on sleeping together when we get back to Cape Town. At most, eighteen months married. We're doing it right, Addi.'

Maybe, Addi thought as she raised her glass to clink it against his beer bottle in a silent toast. But there was still the niggling thought that they could do it better. But life, as she knew, often threw curve balls when you least expected it to.

Jude lay beside Addi, watching her sleep. Beyond her, he could see the dark sea lit by the beam of light coming from a moon mostly hidden behind a thin layer of cloud. The sound of the sea drowned out Addi's soft breaths. He placed a hand on her hip, marvelling at how big his hand looked on her slight body.

It had been a very strange day, and one he was still coming to terms with. While he'd never expected to tell Addi about Marina, he was glad he had. And relieved that she hadn't been anything but empathetic and supportive and hadn't questioned why he'd taken so long to come to the same conclusion about his ex that his grandfather had.

He hadn't explained his need to believe in what he'd assumed he and Marina had had—a connection, a bond, trust—but knew she'd got it. His belief in, and loyalty to, Marina had been the catalyst for so much mistrust and grief in his life. His grandfather had thought him a fool for falling under the spell of a woman, an emotional idiot for not believing his PI's evidence and he'd never let him forget it.

Bartholomew, not a fan of emotion, had second-guessed every decision Jude had made from then on and had never forgiven him for being human. And the story about how Jude had been conned hitting the papers via Jane had been confirmation that his mistrust had been warranted. Jude could, so many years later, still recall Bart's disparaging comments shortly after he'd read the exposé, his mouth lifted in a sneer.

'You're emotional, and you will believe any pretty face with a sob story. Emotion is a weakness, son.

'I don't feel I can trust you with anything more than petty cash,' Bartholomew went on to say. 'You've made some stupid mistakes, ones I can't look past or forgive. And now the whole world knows how stupid you were.'

His grandfather's words, and his disdain, were still burned into Jude's brain and made him writhe with embarrassment and want to run screaming down the beach.

It hadn't occurred to Bart that Jude had been young when he'd fallen for Marina; that hadn't counted. It hadn't mattered that he'd gone on to graduate with a top-class degree or that he'd established a successful side business. Bartholomew had defined him by his mistakes, not his successes. He hadn't wanted to appoint him CEO, but there'd been a Fisher at the helm for over eighty years and he wouldn't let that tradition lapse. But, because he'd considered Jude to be a renegade—an outlier, hot-blooded and impulsive—he'd put those clauses in his will outlining the terms of his inheritance.

His grandfather had been determined not to trust him, to punish him for being less than perfect. But in a year, he'd finally be able to step out of his grandfather's shadow and shed his influence once and for all. He'd gain full control of Fisher International, rid himself of the trustees and make the company his.

One year—all he had to do was to keep the news of his marriage, and the pregnancy, under wraps. He did not want to end up rehashing his past and risking another media embarrassment and a PR headache. In twelve months, he could look forward to a less complicated life.

Most importantly, he would finally be free to make his own decisions, free of Bart's ghost. Free to be who and what he was.

He felt Addi roll over and he looked down into her lovely, sleepy eyes. She lifted her hand to touch his face. 'Are you okay?' she asked, her voice a little groggy. 'It's late. Why aren't you asleep?'

He'd oh-so-casually suggested they have a fling, but it was feeling anything but casual now. And that was dangerous. He lifted his shoulder in a shrug. 'Too much on my mind?'

She tucked her hands under the side of her face. 'Thinking about Marina?'

He hadn't been, actually—or not too much. 'Not really.'

'Good; she's not worth your time.'

Jude stroked his hand over her hair and cupped

his hand around her elegant neck. 'Are we still good, Addi? Still on track?'

A small frown pulled her eyebrows together. 'What do you mean?'

'You won't tell anyone, not even your sister, that we're married, right?'

Irritation and hurt flickered in her eyes. 'I said that I wouldn't, Jude,' she snapped.

He thought about explaining that he had a right to be mistrustful of people—Marina, Jane and his grandfather had screwed him over— but knew she wouldn't appreciate the reminder. He just had to pray she'd stick to her word. The stakes were too high for either of them to mess up now. They just had to keep their mouths shut and all would be well.

Addi rolled over and put a healthy amount of distance between them. He could tell she was angry, that she hated his lack of faith in her—it vibrated off her in waves so strong he could almost see the shimmer in the air. He didn't want to fight with her, not tonight. So he leaned over and placed a kiss on the spot where her neck met her shoulder, loving her scent.

'Sorry,' he murmured.

She didn't turn over. 'You need to trust someone at some point, Jude.'

She didn't understand. And she wouldn't unless he explained that she was asking for the impossible. He rested his forearm over his eyes and wondered where to start. His relationship with Jane was actually harder to talk about than Marina, possibly because he'd been older when it happened, and he should have known better.

'After the Marina incident, I left South Africa, went to the UK and enrolled in the London School of Economics. That's where I met Cole. I thought it would be a fresh start, that no one would be interested in me. Unfortunately, my grandfather was an internationally famous businessman and people paid interest.'

'By "people", you mean the press?' Addi said, turning to face him.

'Yes. Because he was so vociferous in his views, so uncompromising about his values and had a habit of lecturing anybody and everybody he met, many people, especially journalists, wanted to see his feet of clay. But, as hard as they looked, they couldn't find any dirt on him.'

'So they turned their attention to you.'

'I think they sussed, somehow, that my failures would be a thorn in his side. But I'd realised that already.' He dropped his arm and tucked his hand behind his head. 'I kept a very low profile. I had few friends and Cole was one of my best. After six months, the press realised that I was boring and moved on. I graduated, joined Fisher International and ran the company's international interests from London for five years. My grandfather and I worked better together when we lived a continent apart.'

Addi sat up and crossed her legs, her elbows on her knees, her eyes steady on his face. 'I started seeing someone—Jane—after uni, and we were together for a couple of years. I thought that I could put Marina behind me, that it was a youthful misjudgement. I was older, better and wiser. Jane moved in with me and we lived together for a year, maybe a bit more. She worked in finance in the city, and was hugely ambitious, but she had no sense of fair play. Her actions started to worry me. I wasn't comfortable with how she conducted business, and there seemed to be no lines she wouldn't cross.'

Addi pulled a face and a wave of embarrassment swept through him. 'I know how to pick them, right?' he asked, trying to sound upbeat but missing by a mile.

Addi didn't comment, and he didn't see any judgement on her face. 'I found out that she'd slept with her boss for a promotion. Fidelity was, is, important to me, so I told her it was over. She told me that I was overreacting, that it wasn't a big deal.'

'But it was to you.'

She got it. Jude nodded.

'I asked her to move out and she wasn't happy

being downgraded from a penthouse apartment to what she called "a poky flat at the end of the world". It wasn't—she rented a flat on Canal Walk, one of the most expensive areas in the city—but it wasn't Knightsbridge. She begged to come back, said she was sorry, but I was done, you know?'

'Mmm…' Addi nodded. 'What did she do then?'

Sometimes he forgot how smart she was, how she could connect dots at the speed of light. Jude dropped his eyes and looked past her. 'One night, a while before we broke up, after a party and having far too much to drink, I'd told her about Marina and explained how I was played. Jane later sold the story to the press, telling them that I was a terrible partner and that I was cold and unfeeling. She also said that I had a terrible relationship with my grandfather. That, admittedly, was true. She also pointed out that my grandfather didn't trust me and was unhappy about passing the company on to me. Cue share prices dropping, shareholder uneasiness.'

Addi lifted her hand to her mouth, obviously horrified. 'What a horrible woman!' she snapped, her voice hot with anger.

'A few months later my grandfather died, and I discovered he'd added some codicils to his will, hoops I had to jump through, the biggest of which was that a board of three trustees had to approve all my Fisher Holding decisions for ten years. There were also clauses in the will about my behaviour and what he expected from me.'

'Well, obviously I know about the fact that you can't have an illegitimate child, but what else?'

Jude rubbed the back of his head, mentally translating the legalese into everyday language. 'No drugs, gambling, illegitimate kids. I'll only gain full control of the business next year, shortly after you give birth.' He pushed his fingers through his hair, feeling on edge, as if he was walking a tightrope over a thousand-foot canyon.

'I'm surprised nobody knows about the board of trustees,' Addi commented. 'How have you managed to keep them a secret?'

'My grandfather insisted they sign a non-disclosure agreement, which I tightened up after I took over. I also pay them a huge yearly stipend as an added inducement to keep quiet. And we've fallen into a pattern over the years: I only ever consult them when there are massive decisions to be made. They couldn't be bothered with approving the day-to-day decisions; it would adversely affect their golf game.'

Addi flicked her thumbnail against her bottom lip. 'I now understand your reluctance to trust anyone a little better—it's because you've been badly burnt twice.'

'Three times, if you include my grandfather, who couldn't forgive me for misjudging Marina.'

'Your hatred of the press and your wanting to keep a low profile now makes sense. You don't want to rake up old stories.'

He also didn't want Addi to be tainted by the shouted questions, their demands for information, their nosiness and by the press putting their spin on a situation they didn't understand. This was between them; nobody else had a right to comment on what they had.

Whatever it was…

A repeat of being hounded by the press would be a nightmare scenario. He'd spent the past nine-and-a-half years keeping his head down, avoiding anything and everyone that would make headlines, and he had no intention of reliving that awful experience. He didn't want Addi to experience it either.

Neither did he want to be conned again, be betrayed, be screwed over.

Life had been so much easier when he'd lived it solo. But now he had a baby on the way, so that was impossible.

Maybe. Yes, Addi was the one person he trusted more than anyone else. Not fully, not yet—he didn't know if he could ever get there with anyone—but more than he had with anyone for a long, long time. It was a strange, weird, exciting thought. And one he shouldn't be having.

'I still think you should trust more, Jude.'

'Trust me'—that was what she'd meant but hadn't said. 'I know,' he murmured. 'I'm trying, Ads.'

I'm trying to trust you.

He felt the tension leaving her body, flowing out of her muscles. Scooting closer to her, he tucked his knees behind hers and placed his hand on her breast. He felt his eyes closing—he was emotionally wiped—but then her nipple spiked in his palm. When she wiggled her butt into his groin, he dragged his thumb across her nipple and felt her breath hitch. She wanted him…

And, man, it felt so incredibly good to be wanted by *her*.

Not only was she lovely, with a body that he wanted to worship on a daily, *hourly* basis, but she was fresh, kind and, well, *good*. She was like a gust of fresh air blowing through his life, dispersing the secrets and the machinations, scattering the shadows.

Addi lifted her arm to grip the back of his neck and he lifted himself so that his mouth could touch hers. It was an awkward position, so he rolled her onto her back and covered her lips with his, sinking into the spiciness of her mouth.

Making love to her was such a revelation, every single time. Sometimes it was hot and fast, filled with laughter, sometimes it was slow and languorous, almost dream-like. He pulled back and pushed her hair back, their eyes connecting and holding.

This woman was magic; she was safety, grace and freedom.

Disconcerted by his wayward thoughts—she was a fling, and it would be over in a few weeks—Jude ducked his head to kiss her again. When his lips connected with hers, he dived into her mouth, wanting the flash and heat of passion to burn away his dreamy thoughts. He didn't want to feel emotional, he wanted to ride the wave of passion and be immolated by their desire. This was about the pleasure they could give each other, not the succour their soul—*his soul*—needed.

Disconcerted, Jude wrenched his mouth off hers and ducked his head to drag his mouth down her neck. He sucked her nipple into his mouth with more desperation than finesse. He needed to stoke the fire, to make them yearn and burn, to be consumed by what their bodies wanted. Sliding his hands between her legs, he slid one finger into her, then another, looking up to see her eyes close and her mouth fall open.

Yeah, she was with him, carried away by the passion. He placed his thumb on her bundle of nerves, loving the sound of her harsh pant, and her 'take me now' moans. She was so close, and so was he. His erection rested next to her hip, hot, hard and demanding, but he needed to watch Addi fall apart first, riding the pleasure he could give her.

Sitting back, he used his other hand to play with her nipple and watched her blue eyes fog over. She was so close. He debated whether to kiss her nipples, but he wanted to watch her come, wanted to watch her body flush as the moment hit her.

He heard her beg him to come inside her, and although he wanted to, desperately, he swiped his thumb across her, her hips lifted off the bed and her pants grew harsher. She was so close...

And so was he. If he didn't find himself inside her, he might just make a mess of the sheets. 'Addi!'

Her eyes flew open at his harsh command, and he loved the way she found it difficult to focus. He'd done that. He'd made this amazing woman cross-eyed with pleasure and it was one of the greatest achievements of his life.

'Addi, I'm going to touch you again and you're going to let go, okay?'

'Need you…' she muttered, her eyes closing.

'Look at me, Addi!'

When her eyes slammed into his, he touched her again, working her sensitive nerves, and curled his fingers inside her. Heat, heart and pleasure slammed into her and, as she released a keening sound, he pulled out of her and slid inside her, moaning when he felt her warm channel grip him. He didn't need to move, to do anything, he just took a breath and let go, riding away on the force of her orgasm.

It was the hottest, most intense sexual experience of his life and Jude didn't know how to deal with it. All he could do was bury his face in her neck and hold on.

CHAPTER NINE

AFTER VISITING FOUR countries in two weeks, Addi was back in Cape Town. She'd been on so many flights lately that she was now a dab hand at moving from Jude's private plane to his waiting car, sliding into the back seat and greeting Jude's driver by name.

Going back to the real world after being spoiled by private-plane travel, five-star hotels and excellent food was going to be a big culture shock.

Addi looked around the swish reception area of Mazibuko, Cowell and Sithole, and shuffled in the leather club chair. She and Jude had flown in yesterday afternoon so that Jude could attend a meeting in Cape Town. Thankfully, she'd also managed to secure an appointment to see her lawyer to discuss the process and the progress, of getting custody of the girls. She also needed to see a doctor for an antenatal check, but wasn't sure she had time to do that on this trip.

Addi heard a door open behind her and turned to see a gorgeous woman step into the reception area. She wore sky-high heels and a stunning lemon-coloured suit.

'Ms Fields? I'm Thandi Ndaba-Green.'

She was the junior partner Addi had been corresponding with. She stood up and shook her hand. 'Hi, it's nice to meet you. I'm looking forward to hearing where we are and what progress you've made.'

Thandi grimaced and Addi frowned. 'Is there a problem?' she asked.

Thandi gestured to the small conference room off the reception area, with its glass walls and door. Addi followed her inside and turned when the door snicked behind them.

'I tried to call you this morning but I couldn't reach you,' Thandi said, crossing her arms across her chest.

Addi winced. 'Sorry, I was in the air. I saw your message but, since I was coming straight here from the airport, I thought returning your call could wait.'

'That was unfortunate because I could've saved you the trip to our offices.'

Addi looked at the conference table and wondered why she hadn't been offered a seat or something to drink. The appointment was scheduled to last for two hours so she'd expected more than to be kept on her feet and spoken to in a tiny office.

'Is there something wrong? Are you not able to meet with me?' she asked, frowning.

'I'm afraid not,' Thandi told her.

'Why?' When Thandi didn't reply, Addi's heart plummeted to her feet. 'Look, if you can't take my case, then I'll take anyone else in the firm. I just need some help.'

'I'd be happy to help you, Ms Fields, I *want* to help you, but I can't do any more work until we receive your retainer.'

Addi tried to make sense of her words because Jude had paid them over two weeks ago. 'The deposit was made into your bank account a while back,' Addi told her, utterly confused.

Thandi shook her head. 'It hasn't been, I'm afraid. Because of the urgency of the situation, I did start work on your case, hoping to see the money come in. When my bosses realised I was working on your case without payment, they were *not* happy.'

'I'm so sorry,' Addi murmured, humiliation coursing through her body. This conversation reminded her of too many from her childhood, of Joelle sweet-talking her way out of the rent being late, or trying to persuade a lover to let them stay at his place a little longer, despite knowing they weren't wanted.

'You now owe the firm a few thousand in fees. And we can't go any further until we receive payment for that work *and* the retainer,' Thandi told her.

'But…but…' Addi felt her stomach clench, wondering how much damage her lawyer's lack of action and response had caused her. She lifted her hand to her mouth and closed her eyes, trying to push down the rising tide of blood-red anger. The main reason she'd married Jude was to fund the cost of the lawyers so that she could keep custody of the girls.

'You have a hearing tomorrow, and you need representation at that hearing. If you don't, you will put your chances for custody in severe jeopardy,' Thandi told her. 'If we do not get the payment in our account, by the close of the day, I cannot represent you.'

It could take time for money to appear in an account so, even if Jude did do a transfer, they might not see it. She racked her brain, feeling like she couldn't breathe.

'To be clear, if I manage to pay you today, someone will be able to represent me tomorrow?' Addi demanded, feeling hot and cold, then *very* cold at the thought of Thandi saying no.

She nodded and Addi's stomach released one of its many knots. She was supposed to fly out to Namibia tomorrow to view three hotels owned by Thorpe Industries. 'Do I need to be at the hearing?'

Thandi shook her head. 'No, actually, it's better if you stayed away. The lawyers will meet with the judge, and we'll be arguing case law and procedure, so you don't need to be there.'

Okay. Addi flicked her thumb nail against her front tooth and tried to figure out a solution. She needed hard cash and the banks would be closing soon. There was only one other option.

'Do you take credit cards?' she asked.

Thandi nodded. 'Sure. We can go through to the finance officer and I'll swipe your card.'

Ha ha, funny.

She didn't have enough credit on any of her cards, or all of them together, to pay the retainer. And, since Jude's promised maintenance hadn't come through—she'd presumed he'd pay her at the end of the month—she had very little in her current account.

He'd promised to pay the lawyers! How could he let her down like this? She'd been so caught up in him, in the sex and being spoiled, that she'd forgotten to follow up on his promises. How stupid was she? People had always let her down and disappointed her but, because she'd been entranced by Jude's kisses, loved being loved by him, she hadn't checked and double-checked as she usually would.

And that it was Jude who'd disappointed her thoroughly was a shock she'd never expected. Somehow she'd thought that he wouldn't, or couldn't. Yet he had, and she was both angry at him and incandescently angry at herself for assuming he would be different. Angry that she felt enough for him to let this get to her on such a visceral level.

Stupid! Stupid! Stupid!

She forced herself to look at Thandi and caught the sympathy in her eyes. She wanted to help, but Addi understood that her hands were tied.

'What time do you close?' she asked.

Thandi looked at her watch. 'Two hours, but our financial lady leaves in an hour.'

She had an hour to get this sorted. An hour to save the girls from going back to Joelle. She was going to kill Jude for this. Hauling in a deep breath, she forced her mouth into something she hoped was a smile. 'Can you give me a few minutes to make some calls?'

Thandi nodded. 'Sure. I'll find you here in fifteen.' Thandi walked away and, when she reached the door, she turned back. 'Can I get you a cup of tea? Coffee?'

She was grateful for the offer, but she knew that nothing would make it down her super-tight throat. 'Thank you but I'm fine.'

Thandi nodded and walked out, closing the door behind her.

As soon as she was out of hearing, Addi yanked her mobile out of her bag and dialled Jude's number. It rang for an interminably long time before going to voice mail. Swallowing down a growl of fury, she dialled the number again, and this time it cut off immediately, suggesting that Jude had killed her call. She knew he was in an important meeting at Fisher International, but her issue was more crucial than *anything* he was dealing with.

After looking up Fisher International's number, she dialled and asked to be put through to Thabo. Jude's right-hand guy immediately picked up his phone. 'Addi, how are you? How was Zanzibar…?'

She cut him off. 'I can't talk, Thabo. I need to speak to Jude.'

'Not possible, Addi. He's in an important meeting and can't be interrupted.'

Addi ground her teeth together. 'You get in there and tell him to take my call. Right damn now.'

'Addi—'

'Thabo, *do it*! This is crucially important, okay?' Addi shouted.

She heard Thabo's assent and gripped the bridge of her nose as she waited to be connected.

If Jude chose to ignore her, she didn't know what she'd do. She didn't have the time to go to Fisher International herself and get back to this office by the time they closed. If Jude didn't take her call, she might lose custody of the girls before they even started the process.

'Addi, what is the problem?' Jude's voice was sharp and irritated in her ear. 'When I ask not to be disturbed it's for a damn good reason! I have the chairman of—'

'I don't care!' Addi interrupted him, her voice rising. 'What I do care about is that I am at my lawyer's offices. There's a hearing they need to attend tomorrow morning on my behalf, but because you haven't paid them their retainer nobody will attend and I might lose custody of the girls on a technicality.'

'Jeez, slow down, I didn't get most of that.'

Addi ground her teeth together. 'Simply, you didn't pay my lawyers and the custody of the girls is at risk.'

Silence greeted her and it took a while for Jude to speak. 'But I did pay...'

His words drifted away and then she heard his low curse.

'I *meant* to pay them and it slipped my mind,' he admitted. He cursed again. 'I can't believe I did that.'

Addi felt tears gathering in her throat and she

swallowed them down. Then she swallowed
again.

'I'm so sorry, Ads,' Jude told her. 'Look, I'll
do a transfer right now,'

She forced the words up her throat. 'A deposit
might only take a day or two to appear in their
account, which will be too late. I need cash or a
credit card. And I need it here in an hour.'

She heard the breath Jude released. 'Okay.
Wait there. I'll send Thabo with the company
credit card.'

Thabo with the company credit card. *Right.*
After messing up, and putting her sisters in jeopardy, Jude couldn't even make the effort to leave
his office and his meeting to come here himself,
to rectify his mistake. He'd told her how important his business was but, up until this point, it'd
never quite sank in. Fisher International was far
more important than her, than her family.

He'd married her for his business, so why was
that a surprise? But somehow she'd thought that
maybe, just maybe, she'd come to mean more to
him—silly her.

She was racking up the stupidity points,
wasn't she?

'Ads…are you there?' he asked.

'Sure,' she replied in a cold monotone. 'Thabo
and the company credit card.'

'He'll leave now and will be with you in forty-five minutes.' Addi heard his instructions to Thabo and could easily imagine Jude handing over the credit card, hearing him saying something about Thabo taking his SUV and that he'd pay any speeding fines Thabo racked up.

'He's left the office, Addi,' Jude told her.

'Okay.'

She heard his sigh. 'Look, I am sorry. I messed up.'

'Yes, you did,' Addi told him before disconnecting the call.

Yep, he'd screwed up.

Badly.

Jude sat in his car outside Addi's house and lowered his window so that he could push the button on her free-standing intercom system. He was going to have to do some serious grovelling and issue a raft of apologies.

His actions could've caused her lasting harm and he owned that. He wasn't used to thinking of other people and, when he did, he did it on his time scale, not theirs. He'd told her he was going to pay the lawyers and he should've done it immediately. By not doing so, it had slipped his mind. Addi had the right to be angry. In fact, if she was anything less than boil-his-head furious, he'd be surprised. All he could do was apologise and do better...

Be less selfish and more thoughtful.

This was one of the problems with being relentlessly single. He'd forgotten how to be part of a team, to consider other people, that his wasn't the only schedule that mattered and that other people's priorities were different. He'd become intensely self-absorbed, and he didn't like it. When he was like this, he reminded himself too much of his grandfather: someone who lived in his own world, whose thoughts, desires and wants were all that mattered.

It wasn't good enough.

'It's not a good time, Jude.'

At the tinny sound of Addi's voice, Jude jolted in his seat and looked through the slats of the gate to the house beyond. There were lights on in the bottom rooms, but the upstairs rooms were dark. He glanced at his watch and saw that it was past nine. He grimaced. The meeting with his investor had only finished an hour ago and, as soon as he'd ushered her out of his office, he'd jumped into his car and headed here.

'We need to talk, Addison,' he told her.

'We can talk in the morning,' Addi told him.

'I'm going to sit here until you let me in, Addi,' he told her.

She mumbled something, a curse or an oath, but the gate did slide open and he parked his car behind Addi's. There was an old hatchback in the other parking space, and he hoped that he wouldn't have to apologise in front of Addi's three sisters. He would, but he'd prefer to avoid that embarrassment if he could.

Jude left his car and walked up to the front door, the legs of his trousers brushing a pot plant that released a lovely smell of lemon. He looked for a doorbell but then the door opened and Addi stood there, dressed in yoga pants, thick socks and a thigh-length jersey, her face pale and her eyes tired.

He'd been pushing her, pushing *them*, hard lately, flying her from hotel to hotel, country to country, and expecting her to hit the ground running when they got there. Their nights had been spent in bed exploring each other's bodies, and some nights they'd only got a few hours' sleep.

Yes, he'd known that he only had a limited amount of time with her, and that when they returned to South Africa they'd have to be a lot more circumspect if they wanted to keep seeing each other—they couldn't spend every night together. But, because she was so very healthy, he tended to forget she was pregnant and needed rest. She could also do without feeling stressed. He'd failed to look after her.

Yes, she was working with him, but she was first and foremost the mother of his child, and his temporary wife. He should be making life easier for her, not harder. As he'd decided earlier, he had to do better, be better.

'Come in,' Addi told him, and he followed her into a small living room dominated by a cream couch covered in a bright-orange throw. Two old wingback chairs were crammed into the corner and an old TV sat on a credenza. Her laptop sat on the couch and he could see, even from a distance, that she'd been working on a spreadsheet, possibly the master spreadsheet he'd demanded, the one that needed constant updating as new data about Thorpe hotels came in.

She was trying to catch up on the work time she'd lost this afternoon by going to her lawyer.

'Are your sisters around?' he asked, wanting to know how circumspect he had to be.

Addi shook her head. 'No, the girls are with Storm in Durban, and Lex is snowed in with Cole at the ski lodge in the Eastern Cape,' Addi, told him, crossing her arms over her chest. Right… and he was sure his friend wasn't complaining about being snowbound with the woman he found endlessly fascinating.

He was allowing himself to be distracted. An empty house—good. Not hesitating, he walked over to her, placed his hands on either side of her face and rested his forehead against hers. 'I am so, so sorry. I messed up and I've been kicking myself all afternoon. Forgive me?'

She pulled back to put some distance between them 'Do you realise that, if I hadn't had a meeting this afternoon, nobody would've attended the hearing tomorrow and I could've lost the girls before we even started to fight for them?'

Shame ran through him, hot and sour. 'I'm sorry, Addi. So, so sorry. Look, I meant to pay them…'

Addi sat down on the edge of a closet chair. 'But you didn't because you had something better, or more important, to do,' she said in a voice that held no emotion. 'Your work is all that matters, Jude. Everything else comes way down the list.'

He couldn't argue with that; Fisher International had been his entire focus for years, so he said nothing. But, in his defence, he'd had a lot more on his plate than usual—a massive business deal, a temporary wife, a stunning lover and a baby on the way.

'The thing is you could've lost me the most important people in my life. But for the grace of God today, two little girls might've gone back to Joelle, who has the attention span of a flea. They could've been facing the childhood Lex and I did, but in a foreign country. Your selfishness and your lack of focus on anything but Fisher International nearly cost me *everything*.'

He'd far prefer it if she yelled at him, or threw

things, but her cold, low, unemotional voice slashed him in two. He'd known humiliation and regret but that was due to things that had been done *to* him.

He'd done this, it was his actions that could've led to huge, terrible ramifications. In his effort to live his life solo, not to allow anyone into his personal, emotional space and to protect himself from being hurt again, he hadn't made time for other people, and didn't consider what they wanted or needed to be important. His 'I'll get to it when I want to' attitude had severely backfired. He'd hurt Addi and his actions had nearly cost her her sisters.

This time, he couldn't blame his grandfather, Marina or Jane…this was on *him*.

He rubbed the back of his neck. 'I am sorry,' he said again, not knowing what else to say.

And he was—desperately so. He'd let her down, disappointed her. He was just another in a long line of people who'd done that to her, and he hated the thought. He'd never meant to, obviously, but he could kick himself for being just another in the long line of people who'd let her down. It wasn't his finest hour. 'I let you down, failed you. I promise I won't do that again.'

She looked up at him and raised her eyebrows. 'That's a huge promise to make, Jude.'

He dropped to his haunches in front of her and

lifted his hand to touch her face. 'I admit I am selfish, that I don't think of much beyond Fisher International, but that will change, Addi. Today was a huge wake-up call.'

He dragged his thumb over her cheekbone, her blue eyes meeting his. 'Will you forgive me? Please?'

Addi closed her eyes but she did push her face into his hand. When she opened her eyes again, he saw resignation in those blue depths, and extreme exhaustion.

Her words confirmed his suspicions. 'I'm too tired to argue with you, Fisher,' she told him. 'Just…don't, okay? Just don't do it again, alright?' she continued.

Let her down? No, he wouldn't. At least, he'd try his very best not to.

Jude stood up and bent down to scoop her into his arms. He sat down on the couch and held her against his chest, his arms wrapped around her. Addi rested her cheek against his chest and, after a few minutes, he heard her sigh and felt her body relax. She yawned and wiggled closer to him, and he suspected her eyes were closing.

He placed a kiss on her hair, wondering why he instantly relaxed when she did, why holding her in his arms was his form of meditation, his way of feeling zen. After what he'd put her through, he didn't deserve to feel this comfortable. At some point, he'd have to stop kidding himself that she was another fling, someone he could easily walk away from. He'd have to face that something was bubbling between them, something potent.

Just not today. He wasn't ready.

'Have you eaten, Ads?' he asked. He'd noticed that her tummy was a little rounder, her breasts a smidgen bigger, but her arms felt scrawnier, her legs thinner.

She shook her head. 'No energy.'

He'd thought as much. While he was tempted to walk her up the stairs, find her bedroom and put her to bed, he knew that she needed sustenance, and that not eating wasn't good for her or the baby. He needed to keep her awake while he made her something. And he hoped there were eggs in her fridge—his culinary repertoire only extended as far as making scrambled eggs on toast.

She'd fall asleep in a hot bath, and if he told her to watch some TV she'd probably do the same.

The only thing that would hold her energy for a decent time, just fifteen minutes, would be to get her to work. He looked at the open laptop.

'I was looking at the spreadsheet earlier and I think there's a formula error on sheet eight,' he lied.

As he expected, Addi sat up, leaned back and frowned at him. 'I don't make formula errors,' she told him firmly.

'Sure looks like you did,' Jude quietly replied. As he'd expected, she scrambled off his lap and sat on the edge of the couch, her back ramrod-straight as she pulled her laptop onto her knees. She muttered something indecipherable, and Jude took the opportunity to walk into her kitchen and inspect the contents of her fridge. There was eggs, cheese, some salsa and rye bread.

He could work with this.

Digging around, he found a pan, oil, a bowl and a whisk. Within ten minutes he managed to pile a plate high with reasonably fluffy scrambled eggs. He buttered some toast, found a fork and walked back into the lounge, to find her sitting cross-legged on the couch and cursing her laptop.

'I can't find an error,' she told him, sounding grumpy.

He shrugged, whipped the laptop away from her and handed her the plate. She took the eggs and looked up at him. 'What's this?'

'If you don't recognise scrambled eggs then I'm far worse at cooking than I thought I was,' he told her. He sat down next to her and nodded at the plate. 'Eat.'

'I'm not that hungry—'

'Addi, eat the eggs,' he told her, his voice hard-ening.

Addi glared at him but lifted a forkful of eggs to her mouth and chewed. Her eyebrows raised and she dug in for some more, alternating be-tween eating the eggs and munching on the bread. Within minutes she'd polished off all the food on her plate. She leaned back and placed a hand on her stomach. 'Feeding me is becoming a habit, Fisher.'

If that was what it took… He pulled the plate out of her hands, put it on the coffee table and stood up, bending down to lift her into his arms. For a tallish woman, she weighed next to noth-ing.

'Have you been to see the doctor yet?' he de-manded, walking her out of the room.

Her eyes met his. 'We've been in and out of the country for the past two weeks, Jude. When would I have had the time?'

'Tomorrow,' he told her. 'We're going to get you to a doctor before we leave for Namibia. Or do you need to be there for the hearing? If you do, we can push the trip back.'

'No, the lawyer doesn't want me there. Not this time,' she replied. She pushed her hair back to squint at him. 'And may I point out that, for millions of years, a woman didn't rush off to see a doctor just because of a pregnancy? They just carried on with their lives and got on with it.'

Sure, but those millions of women weren't under his care and protection—she was. And so far, he'd been doing a really bad job at looking after her. That would change—right now.

'I'm putting you to bed, you're going to get a decent night's sleep and tomorrow I'll find you a doctor,' he told her, his voice suggesting that she not argue.

Her eyes fluttered closed and he saw she was fighting sleep. 'Are you going to stay the night with me?' she asked as they started climbing the stairs.

After everything that had happened today, did she still want him to stay with her? She was so very generous. 'If you want me to, I will,' he said. 'Which bedroom is yours?'

'First on the right,' Addi told him. He kicked the door open to her room, walked her over to the bed and sat her on the edge of it. 'What do you normally sleep in?' he asked. They usually fell asleep naked but tonight wasn't about sex. Or him.

She waved a listless hand at a chair in the corner. 'T-shirt,' she told him.

He reached for a T-shirt and quickly undressed her, ignoring his erection and fighting the temptation to slide his lips over hers. Even though she was exhausted and irritable—admittedly, all his fault—he wanted her and, judging by the desire in her eyes, she wanted him too.

But want would have to take a back seat; tonight was all about what she needed. And that was sleep. He pulled back her duvet and gestured for her to slide under. When her head hit the pillow, he bent down to place his lips on her temple. 'Good night, Ads.'

'You're not going, are you?' she asked.

He shook his head. 'I'll be up later,' he told her. 'Sleep now.'

He was at the door when he heard her speak again. 'There wasn't an error in the spreadsheet, was there? You just did that to keep me awake.'

Instead of answering her, he just smiled and forced himself to walk downstairs.

CHAPTER TEN

NAMIBIA, THE LAST STOP on their tour of Thorpe establishments, was different from what they'd seen before. After the white sands and heat of the coast of east Africa, and the wild animals in Tanzania, the Skeleton Coast of northern Namibia was wild and desolate and had a beauty unlike any Addi had ever seen, or imagined, before. The area consisted of dunes, desert and the sea and, from just looking at the landscape, Addi understood why it was a place to be feared. The beaches were often shrouded with fog and scattered with the remains of countless shipwrecks and whale skeletons. It exuded a sense of danger, but Addi loved it.

It was also freezing.

A massive cold front had moved in from the Antarctic and a low, dense cloud hung out to sea while an icy wind created white horses on a sullen, gunmetal-grey sea. Addi stood on the veranda of their private room in the tiny boutique hotel and looked at the dunes rolling down to the sea.

Africa was such a land of contrasts, she thought. It could be pretty and calm, wild and dangerous, sleepy and exciting.

But Namibia had captured her soul. She'd met Himba women in the north of the country, enjoyed a game-viewing experience in a private game reserve adjacent to the amazing Etosha Game Reserve and they'd even flown into Botswana to a camp on the Chobe River.

But this place, wild and desolate, held her heart in the palm of her hands. Maybe it was because it was at the tail end of their trip, maybe because it was the last place she would be truly alone with Jude, but she felt a soul-deep connection to the Dune House. The thought of leaving it, and going back to her normal life, made her feel a little ill.

Addi felt her phone vibrate and, seeing it was from her lawyer Thandi, pounced on the message.

Hearing done. It went well. No problems, and nothing for you to worry about. Our case is strong. Just waiting for a date for the final hearing in front of the judge.

She heard the sliding door open behind her and turned to look at Jude, who carried two mugs in his big hands. His would be filled with two shots of espresso, hers would be ginger tea, something she'd taken to drinking to ward off the occasional bouts of nausea she experienced throughout the day.

She waved her phone. 'The custody hearing went well. Thandi's waiting for a date for the final hearing,' she told him.

His smile flashed. 'That's really good news, Ads.' He handed her a cup and Addi wrapped her hands around it, enjoying the warmth. She watched the wind lift his hair and when he sucked in a breath she smiled. 'It's freezing, isn't it?'

'It's snowing in numerous places in South Africa. Including at the ski resort where Lex and Cole are holed up,' Jude replied.

Addi nodded. 'I've been getting updates. The girls are furious they aren't anywhere near the snow.' Storm, their middle sister, had scooped up the girls and taken them on holiday to the much warmer east coast of South Africa. 'Storm thought about driving them to where the snow is, but the roads are closed and it's too dangerous.'

She was glad that Lex was having a break from the girls, and she hoped that she was enjoying a rip-roaring affair with Cole Thorpe, their joint boss. She'd sensed the attraction sizzling between them whenever they were together, and Lex deserved some fun.

Thank God for Storm scooping up the younger girls…

'And why are we out here when there's a toasty fire inside?' Jude asked.

Addi gestured to the view. 'Because it's beautiful,' she replied.

This was the last of Cole Thorpe's hotels and they'd be leaving tomorrow. Jude had all the information he needed to decide which properties he wanted and her involvement was no longer necessary.

When they returned to South Africa, they would be forced to act like colleagues, because no one could suspect that they'd been carrying on a rip-roaring, hot-as-Hades affair. They would have to act, look and be professional and she would be going home to her house, he to his.

Where did they go from here? The question was at the front of her mind, and had been since they'd left Cape Town ten days ago, the day after their fight and just a few hours after she'd had her first doctor's visit. The intense feeling that they were on borrowed time was something she couldn't rid herself of.

It was hard to accept that she was in too deep, but the reality was that she'd allowed her feelings to run away from her. If she wasn't already in love with Jude, then she was damn close, and she knew she needed to shore up her defences. She couldn't stop herself from sleeping with him—she was a woman, not a saint—but she needed to protect her heart.

But how? And was it too late?

And why did she feel as if she was on a count-down, as if there was a timer somewhere ready to detonate a bomb in their lives? It had to be because she was worried about the girls and the custody case; it had nothing to do with Jude and their 'out of Africa', oh-so-temporary fling.

She didn't think.

'What do you think of this place?' Jude asked, putting his back to the view. 'It's really small.'

The boutique hotel only had five rooms, was incredibly isolated and required a helicopter flight to reach the hotel. But the building was stunning: a modern, steel-and-wood, open-plan lower floor with glass walls on three sides en-abling the guests to have a one-eighty-degree view of the dunes and endless sea. It reminded her of Jude's house in Franschhoek.

The five double rooms were massive and each had private balconies and hot tubs, fireplaces and enormous beds. Of all the places they'd vis-ited, this was the most stunning.

'Are you asking me to answer professionally or personally?'

'Both. Professionally, first.'

'Well, like the ski lodge Cole and Lex are stuck at, I think this was another passion project by Cole's father. It's booked solid in spring and summer but the place empties in autumn and winter. It's covering its costs, just, but you are never going to make money from it.'

Jude's eyes slammed into hers. 'And personally?'

'It's…' She hesitated, unsure about how to explain. She didn't have the words to tell him that, from the moment she'd left the helicopter and looked through the dunes to the sea, she'd felt captivated. That she could walk the desolate beach for hours at a time and feel rejuvenated, that it was an almost spiritual experience to be here.

She chewed on her bottom lip. 'I think this is the place where my soul feels most at home,' she quietly admitted.

He didn't respond to her comment, and after twenty seconds she risked looking at him to see his eyes on her face. 'That sounds, weird, right?' she lifted her shoulders to her ears. 'I don't know how else to explain it but, every time I look out to sea, when I walk that wooden slatted path to the beach, I feel like I am home.'

Jude lowered his eyebrows and nodded. 'It's

a pretty special place but I did not expect you to feel so strongly about it.'

She didn't understand it either. She loved her home, but it was noisy and chaotic, filled with girls fighting, laughing or yelling. This place was pure serenity.

She shook her head and lifted her mug to her lips again. She was being silly, that was all. This wasn't where she belonged; she'd never return to this place again.

Real life wasn't isolated houses on a desolate beach, days and nights spent with the sexiest, smartest man she'd ever known. It wasn't flitting about in private planes and having five-star experiences at some of the best places on the continent. It wasn't making love outdoors on blankets in front of fires while the cold wind roared outside, or in hot tubs while elephants strolled past a private chalet. It wasn't running into the warm Indian ocean late at night or early in the morning, swimming with wild dolphins or sleeping in treehouses.

Real life was in Cape Town, behind her desk at Thorpe Industries—or at another corporation, maybe Fisher International. It was growing and birthing this baby. It was telling Lex and the girls that she was going to be a mother—God, she hated keeping secrets from them—and figuring out how to let Jude be a part of their baby's life.

'Are you okay?' Jude asked, placing his hand on her arm. 'You look a little pale.'

'Just cold,' Addi told him. 'There's a fire inside, why are we standing out here?'

'I said that ten minutes ago,' Jude pointed out as he followed her inside. Addi walked up to the freestanding fireplace and held her freezing hands out to the flames. She sighed when Jude wrapped his arms around her waist and rested his chin on her hair.

'Are you sure you're okay, Ads?'

No.

But she nodded, glad he couldn't see the tears welling in her eyes. Yes, of course she was. She had no choice *but* to be okay. She was responsible for herself and for three other people—and a half—and nobody was going to ride to her rescue and patch her up, prop her up.

No, she was used to being alone, doing alone. And when they returned to Cape Town tomorrow that was exactly what she'd do.

This was it; they were home.

Their out-and-about-in-Africa fling was over.

Jude's jet rolled to a stop and Addi pulled her seat belt apart, grimacing at the wet and windy weather outside the plane's small, oval window.

She wished she was back in Zanzibar or Turtle Bay, swimming in the lukewarm sea and wearing flip-flops. She far preferred summer to winter, though to be honest making love in front of a fire yesterday, while the wind had wailed and roared around Dune House, hadn't been a problem.

Jude leaned forward, looked past her and grimaced. 'They say that this has been the wettest and coldest winter in decades.'

Yep, let's talk about the weather, because that's what's important, Addi thought.

'At least there isn't as much snow with this system,' Addi replied, pulling her bag off the seat in front of her. Her floppy felt hat lay on top of it and she pulled it on, as well as a voluminous scarf. The weather was easy to discuss, and far less explosive than asking what their relationship would look like going forward from this point on. A bunch of other questions hovered on her tongue.

When would she see him again, make love to him again? Was this *it*? They'd inspected all the properties; they'd had their affair. Now that they were back in Cape Town, they were going to have to be a lot more circumspect, act as if they barely knew each other, that they were no more than work colleagues. And that was going to be hard. She was so used to taking his hand, snuggling into his side when he put his arm around her, sharing her bed and her body.

She didn't know how to act, or what to say.

'All you need is big sunglasses and you'll look like an A-list celebrity who's trying to look like she doesn't want the attention but secretly does,' Jude commented.

Addi poked her tongue out at him, then wrinkled her nose, thinking she was no more mature than Nixi or Snow.

'What are your plans today?' Jude asked, standing up as the engines faded away. He lifted his arms to stretch, his cashmere jersey pulling flat against his wide chest.

'Well, I want to spend some time with Lex, to reconnect with her. I have to tell her about the baby, obviously, and about Joelle seeking custody of the girls.' His mouth opened and she knew he was going to remind her not to say anything about their marriage. *Really? Again? 'Don't*, Jude.'

He nodded, looking resigned. 'Are you happy about her and Cole?'

'How can I not be?' she asked him. Lex being Cole's chauffeur and then being snowbound in a ski lodge he owned had led them to fall in love. She'd been the first person Lex had called when Cole had proposed, and they'd spent hours on video call catching up. That Cole loved Lex was indisputable and Addi was so happy for, and maybe a little jealous of, her younger sister. Lex was incandescently happy. And that was all that mattered.

'She wants to show me the new house Cole has bought. She's also asking if I'm interested in moving into their guest house.'

Cole had bought Lex a massive property that would house all the sisters in individual houses, allowing Nixi and Snow to run from the main house where they'd live to her cottage and the above-garage apartment they'd allocated to Storm.

Jude's gaze pinned her feet to the floor of the plane. 'Are you? Interested, that is?'

She shrugged. 'I haven't even seen the place, Jude! And I love my house, it's home. And I'm not sure I want to live on my soon-to-be brother-in-law's property. I'm far too independent for that.

'Lex and I have so much to talk about! She's going to rip my head off for keeping so many secrets,' Addi continued.

Jude pushed his hands into the pockets of his grey trousers. 'Lex marrying Cole will be a big boost to your custody suit. His name is as big as mine. If it gets that far, I don't know if you are going to need to name me in the papers.'

Addi knew he was worried his name would be

leaked if they got before the judge. Her lawyers had agreed to keep quiet the fact that they were married, and that Jude would only be brought into the conversation if all other means to obtain custody of the girls fell through. His involvement was a last resort, a nuclear option. But, now that Cole was marrying Lex, Jude's influence might not be needed, especially as the girls would be moving into his house with Lex.

Addi understood that Jude didn't want his business to be front-page news again. But a part of her—the silly, tender, romantic smidgeon of her soul—wanted him to say that he'd walk through fire for her, endure months of being fodder for gossip for her. She was falling in love with him—*was* in love with him—and a part of her wanted him to make the grand gesture, to defend her, to move mountains for her. Not to care what the world thought…

You're forgetting that this is a business arrangement, Addi, that there is nothing between you but a baby and great sex. Your fling is over.

'After I tell her about the custody battle, I'll need Lex to come with me to meet Thandi so she can get up to speed on the case,' Addi told him. 'I imagine that, as soon as Cole hears about Joelle's latest scheme, he'll offer to pay for the lawyer's costs.'

'I'm paying for it, that was part of *our* deal,' Jude snapped.

She wasn't prepared to argue with him, not right now. 'Lex will be furious with Joelle, but she'll probably be a lot less worried about winning custody than I am. Lex is far more optimistic than I am.'

'I think the chances of a judge siding with your neglectful mother against three sisters who are raising two happy and healthy little girls is minimal. I don't think there's much to worry about,' Jude told her.

But it was her job to worry, her job to ensure that their family was safe and protected. 'I'll relax when I see the court order, when Lex and I are named their guardians.'

'You have to have a little faith, Addi.'

He was saying *that* to her? This was the person who'd reminded her, twice yesterday and three times today, that they couldn't be linked together, that she couldn't say anything about them being married, variations on the 'this can't hit the papers' spiel. If he mentioned the words 'press' and 'secret' one more time, she might brain him.

He had no concept of faith or trust. He'd made up his mind that no one could be trusted and that included her. And that made her eyes well up and her heart sink to the floor because, without trust, there couldn't be love.

And, because she was intensely stupid when it came to matters of the heart, she'd fallen in love with him.

Stupid, stupid girl.

Addi turned away and scrabbled in her bag, using it as an excuse not to look at Jude. If he saw her eyes, he'd see the longing, the love, her hopes and dreams about their future on her face and blazing in her eyes. A house of their own, two little girls running in and out, a baby to raise and a man in whose arms she could rest at night, whose face she wanted to kiss for the rest of her life... A friend to talk to, a steady partner willing to share the responsibilities life continuously shoved her way, someone steady and reliable.

And hot.

There was something to be said for sharing her life with someone who could make her insides quiver, her knees melt and her breath hitch.

Except that she wouldn't.

There was no chance of living her life with him, raising a baby and sharing the ups and down. They would stay secretly married for another year and a bit, then they'd quietly divorce, hopefully without anyone being any the wiser. Their baby would be raised in separate houses and they'd share custody. Their sole link would be through their child…

She was weaving dreams from fairy dust, and that wasn't like her. She didn't dream or hope, she faced life as it was; living with Joelle had taught her to do that. She had to look at life the way it was, not how she wanted it to be.

Jude would never love her. She had to accept and deal with that. And soon.

'I wonder what's causing the delay,' Jude said. Addi turned to look at him and saw his frown. He bent down to push the intercom to talk to his pilot. 'Siya, what's the problem?'

'Sorry, boss, there's been a breach in security, someone tried to sneak through onto the taxi-way. He's been arrested but they aren't allowing private cars up to the planes.'

Jude pulled a face. 'Does that mean we have to go through arrivals?'

'Yes, sorry, sir. An Airports Company representative will be with us shortly and he'll escort you to the terminal.'

'I know where to go, Siya,' Jude told him.

'Airport rules, sir. Joe is going to open up and drop the stairs. He'll follow with your luggage.'

'Okay, thanks, Siya.' Jude reached for his black leather jacket and pulled it on. When he looked at Addi, his expression was impenetrable.

'Okay, so we're going to have to walk through the terminal. Remember, we are—'

'Work colleagues, people who barely know each other. We can't give anyone the impression that we are married or lovers or even friends!' Addi snapped. 'I have a degree in business management, Jude, you don't need to keep reminding me or treating me like an idiot.'

'I'm not, I'm just reminding you...'

Addi saw the cockpit door open and held up her hand, cutting off Jude's words. It took all her energy to smile at Joe. 'Thanks for ferrying us around safely these past few weeks, Joe. Will you thank Siya for me too?'

'Certainly,' Joe replied, before turning his attention to the door. He opened it and cold air drifted into the plane as Addi pulled her bag over her shoulder and picked up her laptop case.

Jude gestured for her to precede him, and she realised that the temperature between them had plummeted. And not only because of the cold front currently battering the city.

Okay, maybe he'd been a bit heavy-handed earlier. He hadn't needed to keep reminding Addi about their agreement, that their arrangement couldn't become public knowledge.

Maybe he was just reminding her to remind himself, to convince himself that there was nothing between them but great sex and a baby on the way.

He wasn't making any progress on that front.

The thing was…he liked her. He *like* liked her.

Jude jammed his hands into the pockets of his jacket and rolled his eyes, irritated with his juvenile assessment of the situation. How old was he—fifteen?

He loved making love to Addi, it had quickly become his favourite thing to do. But he also enjoyed her sharp mind, and understood her sometimes prickly attitude—she was her family's protector and life had taught her to fight. And he enjoyed seeing the softer side to her, the Addi behind the shields. That woman was lovely and warm, funny and fantastic, and he didn't know how he was going to live his life without her constant presence.

Jude felt the cold wind slide down his back as they hurried across the apron, and he yanked his hand from his pocket to rest it on Addi's back but pulled back at the last minute. He couldn't touch her; he couldn't act or be solicitous. At the remote locations they'd recently visited, privacy and isolation had been high on the list of the hotels' offerings, so he hadn't been worried about their connection being revealed.

But here in Cape Town, where everyone had a

mobile phone and could snap a photo, they had to be extremely careful.

Understanding that, how were they going to carry on seeing each other? They had maybe another two weeks of using the guise of working together to hide behind but, after that, once he put in an offer to buy Cole's properties, that excuse would disappear, along with her job. Once she moved across to Fisher International, it would be even harder. Along with coffee, gossip was the lifeblood of his company.

And gossiping about him was his employees' favourite sport. Jude made a mental note to contact his Human Resources director about Addi's appointment, something he had yet to take care of.

He shook his head at his lack of efficiency, shocked that, like paying the lawyers, it had slipped his mind. He rarely forgot to complete items on his to-do list, and the few things he did forget were ridiculously unimportant. Nothing had dropped through the cracks before Addi had entered his life—he hadn't even *had* cracks. But, since she'd fallen into his life the second time, he'd felt consistently off-balance and discombobulated. She turned him inside out and upside down in a way he'd never experienced before.

His mind was a mess, he thought, as he gestured for Addi to precede him into the airport terminal. They followed an airport staff member to a passport control desk with no queue, and an officer who stamped their passports, barely taking the time to check their photos against their faces. Normally, the customs official would come to the plane but, judging by the fact that every security officer he could see looked to be on high alert, their heads swivelling back and forth, the security breach had been bigger than expected.

The customs official touched his hat and gave Jude a sympathetic smile.

What was that for?

Jude started to weave his way between the other passengers, making sure Addi stayed by his side. They bypassed the conveyor belts spitting out luggage and headed toward International Arrivals. It was then that Jude realised that he'd lost his escort. Shrugging it off, because he knew the way, he kept walking, wondering why the hair on the back of his head was lifting.

What was he missing here?

The automatic doors opened and as they stepped over the threshold into the terminal what seemed a million cameras exploded simultaneously. Out of the corner of his eye, he saw Addi raise her hand, and he moved to stand closer to her, his body half-shielding her from the crowd gathered behind the cordon.

'Why did you get married, Jude?'

'Why her?'

'Who is she?'

'Any thoughts on what your grandfather would think about who you married?'

'Would he approve this time?'

How? What? How had they found out?

Knowing that he had to keep his head, Jude sent the crowd a blistering glare and placed his hand low on Addi's back, edging her towards the exit. In six feet, maybe a little more, they would be surrounded, and he'd have to push his way through the crowd, somehow keeping his grip on Addi.

How had this happened? How had they found out? And how was he going to get them out of here? At that moment, Jude felt as he had ten years ago, intensely betrayed and awash with humiliation. He didn't feel like the man who owned and operated a highly successful company, didn't see himself as the powerful hotel whizz-kid everyone regarded him to be. No, he was ten years younger again, withering as his grandfather had ridiculed his actions.

He could hear Bart's voice mocking him, his voice more derisive than ever before.

You thought you had it together, didn't you? Not so smart, are you? Another scandal, another embarrassment. Yet another misjudgement. Are you ever going to learn, son?

Knowing he couldn't keep looking like a deer caught in the headlights—not a look he wanted to be splashed across papers and on news websites—he gripped Addi's hand tightly and steered her left. He could beat himself up later for failing to anticipate this, for making the mistake of trusting Addi. Right now, they had no choice. They had to go forward.

And suddenly, without fuss, six men dressed in black suits, and looking as though they shouldn't be messed with, stepped in front of the journalists and flanked them, creating a barrier between them and the screeching journalists.

Grateful for their presence, Jude caught the eye of the guy to his left as they forged a path to the airport. 'Who sent you?' he asked. He had his suspicions, but he wanted to have them confirmed.

'Cole Thorpe.'

As he thought. Thado was overseas and Cole was the only person who knew what time they were landing and had been around when the stories about him being conned by Marina had made headlines. He needed to send him a case of his shockingly expensive favourite whiskey for sending in the cavalry.

'Am I right in presuming that this story broke within the last couple of hours?'

The bodyguard nodded. 'There's a car in the pick-up zone, waiting to take you wherever you want to go.'

A reporter managed to jump between one of the bodyguards to take an up-close photograph of Addi, with her wide eyes and panicked face. He was tossed back into the crowd by one of their bodyguards and Addi looked at him, her face pale with apprehension. 'What's happening, Jude?'

'We've been ambushed by the press, Addison,' he quietly replied in his coldest voice. 'That's what happens when you can't keep a secret. Did you do it as pay-back because I forgot to pay the lawyers?'

She braked and, oblivious to the interest from everyone around them, placed a hand on his arm to halt his fast progress across the terminal. '*What?* Do you think *I* did this? That I broke my promise to you?'

'Well, *I* didn't,' Jude snapped back.

'Not now,' the senior bodyguard snapped, and Jude cursed himself for losing his cool and control. He placed his hand on her back and propelled her forward. He turned to look at her face, grimacing when despair shot across her face and anguish settled in her eyes. They could discuss the hows and whys later; right now they had to get out of there.

They hit the outside doors and Jude let out a sigh of relief when he saw the two black SUVs parked in the pick-up zone. *Excellent.* He ducked into the SUV first, climbing across the bench seat to make space for Addi, and when she failed to climb in after him he whipped around to see her veering left and sliding into the second SUV.

And, since the press corps had followed them out of the terminal onto the pick-up zone, his only choice was to let Cole's private security drive them away in separate cars.

CHAPTER ELEVEN

ADDI BEGGED THE bodyguards to drop her at her cottage and, when they told her they had orders to take her to Jude's Franschhoek residence, she pitched a fit. She didn't want to go there with him, and if they took her anywhere against her will it would be kidnapping.

After some quiet, undiscernible conversations, Addi noticed the change of direction of the car and within forty minutes she was in her house, pacing the space next to her kitchen table. It was mid-morning, the girls were at school and she assumed Lex was with Cole. She had the house to herself, and she desperately needed the quiet and the space.

She needed time to think, to plan, to pick her shattered heart off the floor and reinsert it into her chest. She knew Jude had trust issues, and understood why he couldn't open up and trust anybody, but his first instinct when he'd seen the press had been to blame her for the news about their secret marriage getting out.

He hadn't been prepared to consider other options, nor consider alternatives to how the news of their marriage could've been leaked. His first instinct had been to assume she was to blame.

But what hurt even more, what had her wanting to curl up in a ball and howl, was that he considered her to be as vengeful and vicious as Marina and Jane, that she was vindicative enough to seek pay-back for a mistake he'd made and apologised for. That he didn't rate her higher than the two women who'd betrayed him cut her to every bone.

Standing in her kitchen, Addi finally accepted that he would never trust her, and without trust he could never love her. Not the way she needed him to.

They'd spent so much time together, weeks of laughing, loving and confiding, but their supposed closeness meant nothing to him, it didn't make a jot of difference. She'd been hurt before, by Joelle and Dean, but nothing hurt as much as Jude's instinctive, absolute distrust.

Addi pulled out a chair from under the dining table and dropped into it, resting her throbbing head in her hands. What were they going to do now? How was she going to handle this?

And, she thought, picking up her head, where

was her luggage? A bodyguard had taken her laptop and handbag from her when they'd surrounded her at the airport and he'd slid into the same vehicle as Jude, assuming that was where she'd go. As a result, she didn't have her phone or her laptop and had no means of communication. Thank goodness they had a code system on the front door and their gate, as well as being able to open it with a remote, or else she wouldn't have been able to get into the house.

Addi stood up and walked around the table to switch on the kettle. She needed a cup of tea and to think, and it would help if she could stop crying. Yes, a little part of that was shock. Being half-blinded by camera flashes and deafened by shouted questions had not been a fun experience. And that guy popping up in front of her had scared her, so she had a right to feel shaky. She would be fine after a cup of tea and a few deep breaths.

Getting over the fact that Jude didn't trust her, not even a little bit, that he thought her treacherous, would take a lot longer.

Addi poured water over a teabag and frowned when she heard her front door open and close. She hastily rubbed her fingers over her eyes, picking up tears and wiping them on her dark-green skinny jeans. Lex was back and, while she was looking forward to reconnecting with her sister, she'd wanted a little more time to compose herself before they spoke. Lex would've seen the papers and would have questions about her marriage. She also needed to tell her about the baby and the custody battle, and she wanted to be calm and in control when she did so.

Addi waited to hear her footsteps coming into the kitchen, for her to call out, but when neither happened she frowned and, picking up her cup, walked into the hallway…to see Jude standing there, her suitcase at his feet. He held her laptop bag and tote bag in a tight grip.

She most certainly wasn't ready to deal with Jude Fisher. 'What are you doing here and how did you get in?' she demanded.

He kicked her suitcase with the side of his foot. 'Delivering your stuff. If you'd got into the same car as me, I wouldn't have had to follow you here,' he shot back, looking angrier than she'd ever seen him.

'I *never* asked you to do that. And you didn't answer my question about how you got into my house.'

'I called Lex. She gave me the code. She also bombarded me with questions about our marriage and what we thought we were doing.'

'Well, I wasn't the one who asked for secrecy, was I?' Addi retorted.

Jude grimaced as he placed her laptop bag on

top of her suitcase and hung her tote bag up on a hook behind her door. Addi heard the strident ring of her phone coming from the handbag.

'That's probably her now,' Jude told her, removing his leather jacket.

'What did you tell her?' Addi demanded. She'd lose it if he'd told her about the baby. He knew how important it was for her to tell Lex that news herself.

Jude gave her a sour look. 'Nothing. I told her you would answer all her questions.' Jude placed his hands on his hips and looked around. 'Are we going to fight in your hallway?'

Addi narrowed her eyes. 'We might as well,' she told him.

'Why are you so mad at *me*?' Jude demanded. 'And why did you get into another car?'

Seriously? Had he really asked her that? 'You accused me of leaking the story!' she yelled. 'You said that I revealed our secret!'

'Well, I didn't, so how else did they get to hear about it?' Jude yelled back. He shrugged and spread out his hands. 'Look, I know how close you and Lex are, I know that you don't keep secrets from each other, so I understand why you told her. She probably let it slip that we were married to someone—'

'I didn't tell anyone!' Addi screamed, hoping that a little volume would get her message across. 'And don't you think that Lex asking you all those questions about our getting married is a clue that she *didn't* know?'

He frowned, started to speak and shook his head, his frown deepening. She saw a bank-load of pennies drop and Jude ran his hands over his face. 'Right, well… I didn't think that through. Sorry.'

Addi threw up her hands, frustrated beyond belief. One sorry—was that it? Oh, he had to be joking. She slapped her hands on her hips. '*No!* No, you don't get to come in here after slinging such a nasty accusation and, on realising you were wrong, fob me off with a simple "sorry". I'm *not* accepting that.

'And, even if I could get past that—and I can't—how dare you accuse me of leaking the news of our marriage as pay-back for a mistake you made and apologised for? I am not that vindicative or nasty!'

He shoved an agitated hand through his hair. 'I didn't mean—'

'Don't tell me that it was the heat of the moment, that you weren't thinking—and don't you *dare* tell me you didn't mean it. The thing is, Jude, when the chips are down, when a stressful situation happens, people *do* say what they mean—they tend to tell the truth because they don't have time to parse their words through a

filter. You meant every word you said at that
moment, because you believe instinctively that
I would screw you over. That I am just another
woman out to hurt you.'

He didn't reply and she was glad: she would've
lost respect for him if he'd tried to talk his way
out of what they both knew was the truth. He
just looked at her, misery and a touch of defi-
ance in his eyes.

'Despite spending these past few weeks with
me, despite our conversations and our confes-
sions, you don't trust me any more than when I
first walked into your house and told you about
the baby.'

He folded his arms across his chest and rocked
from foot to foot. 'I've been trying, Addi.'

'But you can't get there.' Cold sadness rolled
over her and it took everything she had not to
drop to her knees and rest her forehead on the
floor. There was no hope for them as a couple,
not even a smidgeon.

She loved him, and he felt something for her,
but it wasn't enough to overcome her fear that
he'd keep disappointing her in big ways and
small. Jude had let her down twice now, and
she did not doubt that, unless he fundamentally
changed his thinking, he'd do it again.

Love couldn't flourish where there was doubt.
The two were mutually exclusive.

Jude rubbed his hand up and down his jaw. 'We've only known each other a short time, Addi. I'm not used to you, not used to this. I've been on my own for a long time and I'll do better.'

I'll do better.

How many times had she heard that from Joelle, and how many times had she disappointed her? Dean had said something similar after their fights about how he couldn't connect with the girls. Neither of them had *done better*.

After not paying her lawyers, Jude had promised not to let her down again, yet here he was. Was she really going to allow the people she loved to keep disappointing her, to allow history to repeat itself?

Didn't she deserve more? Hadn't she promised herself that she would never put herself in this position again?

'The man who wanted to marry me tried to love me enough, but he couldn't get there. I grew up with a woman who promised me more than she could deliver, and who never gave me what I needed and wanted. I kept waiting, kept hoping, and every time she made me a promise and didn't deliver I lost a piece of my soul. I won't do that again.'

Every time Joelle let her down, she lost another chunk of respect and liking for her mother.

She didn't want that to happen with Jude. He was going to be in her life for a long time, they were going to have a child together. She had to stop wanting, stop dreaming, and she definitely had to stop expecting him to be better. It was the only way she could see them having any type of relationship going forward.

She sucked in some air and forced down her tears. She could, and most definitely would, cry later.

'We were going to re-evaluate our relationship anyway, so let's just call us done, Jude,' she told him, forcing the words over her suddenly thick tongue. 'Let's just live our separate lives, you in your house, me in mine. After the baby is born, we can get a divorce. All I need you to do is pay for the lawyer's fees, as per our initial arrangement.'

'But—what about us?' Jude asked.

'There is no *us*, Jude! There can't be an *us* because you can't give me what I need.'

'And what is that, Addi, exactly?' Jude asked, his voice low and growly with suppressed emotion. Anger or despair? She couldn't tell. 'Spell it out for me.'

'I need you to love me! I need you to be part of my life, and our baby's life, on a daily basis. I want to grow old with you and love you every minute between now and then. Because—and I hate this—I love you, Jude.'

He started to reach for her, but Addi knew that, if he touched her, her resolve would melt like sugar strands on a hot stove plate.

'But me loving you isn't enough for me. I did that with my mother, and it nearly killed me.'

'I *could* love you, Addi.'

She looked into his confused eyes and shook her head. 'I don't think you can, Jude, because you can't trust me. And because you can't put me first, ahead of Fisher International. I refuse to be the little girl I was, trailing behind the shooting star, praying that now and again you'll look back and remember that I'm there. I've done that, it's not fun. I'd rather live without you—and I *can* live without you—than be anything less than your everything.'

'You're asking for a lot, Addi,' Jude said, his eyes narrowing.

She lifted one shoulder in a desperate shrug. She wished he would leave. She desperately wanted to cry, but she wouldn't, not when he was there. 'Maybe. Maybe I should be grateful to get whatever you decide to give, but I'm not that type of girl. Like my sisters, I deserve a guy who will make me his entire world. And, if you can't be that man, then I would rather be alone.'

Jude dropped his head to look at the floor and

Addi brushed past him to pull open her front door. 'Please go, Jude. If you love me a little, if you just harbour a little affection for me, go. Go before I stop being brave.'

Jude turned round, walked towards the door and stopped next to her. He leaned down and Addi tensed, hoping he wouldn't kiss her. He hesitated but pulled back. 'I'm so sorry I can't give you what you need, Addi. The level of trust you require is impossible for me.'

'I know,' Addi whispered.

As she watched him walk to his car, tears rolled down her face and dripped off her chin. Yep, watching someone she loved walk away wasn't getting any easier.

Lex sat cross-legged on the couch next to Addi, horror and sympathy in her eyes. She held a large glass of wine in her hands and Addi was tempted to wrench it out of her grasp and knock it back. She needed the soothing properties of the fermented grape.

'How far along are you?' Lex asked.

'Eleven, twelve weeks?' Addi replied, wrinkling her nose. It was difficult to think. Her head felt like it was stuffed with cotton wool and her heart was anvil-heavy in her ribcage. On the big screen in her mind, she kept watching Jude walk away, devastation in his eyes.

Had she been too tough on him? Had she acted too hastily? Had she not given him enough time to learn to trust her—had she expected too much?

She missed him. She missed him so much that even her hair was hurting...

'When are you going to have your first scan?' Lex asked.

'I don't know,' she admitted. She waved a listless hand. 'Some time.'

'Ads, you are the most together person I know, and the fact that you don't know, to the hour, how far along you are or when your next appointment is concerns me. I'd expected you to have made six lists, booked Lamaze classes and started investigating schools.'

She'd get back to being her organised self soon. Right now, she was just trying to keep her heart and soul together, and she didn't have the energy to be a control freak. 'I'm sorry I fell pregnant, Lex. I'm sorry I messed up.'

Lex pulled back to look at her, her lovely face shocked. 'Why are you apologising to me?'

'We made an oath. We said that we wouldn't follow in Joelle's footsteps.'

'Oh, Ads, you are so hard on yourself.' Lex put her wine glass on the coffee table and lifted her hand to stroke her hair. 'I know that you were on the pill and that Jude probably used a condom. This little munchkin—' Lex pushed the tip of her finger into Addi's stomach —'obviously wanted to be here. She fought past two contraceptives to be here. God, she's a warrior.'

'She could be a boy,' Addi murmured.

Lex grinned. 'No, she's a girl. We only make girls, Ads.' She rubbed her hand over Addi's belly. 'I'm so excited to meet the newest member of our clan, Ads. You are going to be such a great mum.'

Addi shook her head. 'I'm not so good with Nixi and Snow, not as good as you.'

Lex shook her head. 'Addi, you were working, trying to make money to keep us fed and clothed and safe. You were exhausted. You don't have to be *everything* to everybody.'

Jude had said the same. And maybe it was time to give herself a break, to accept that she'd done the best she could with the resources she had, mental, physical and financial, and move on. Everyone was fine…

Well, she wasn't, but her sisters were.

'I'm still mad you didn't tell me about the baby and the legal battle earlier, Addison.'

Addi winced. 'I was trying to spare you the stress.'

'Ads, I'm not a little girl any more and you don't need to protect me,' Lex told her. 'I'm your sister, an adult, and I deserve to be treated as one.'

Addi scrunched up her face, knowing she was right. It wasn't her job to protect Lex any more, to look after her. She was perfectly capable of looking after herself and it was time she backed down and away. 'I know. And I'm sorry.'

Luckily, Lex didn't hold grudges. 'Cole told me that it was the priest who leaked the news of your marriage to the press, by the way. He sold the story, but only after Jude's fat donation hit his bank account.'

Addi's mouth fell open. Well, that was one mystery solved. 'The greedy pig!'

Lex nodded her agreement. 'So, we have a custody hearing the day after tomorrow, and Joelle will be there. Cole and Storm will join us and, if we show a united front, Thandi doesn't think the judge will give Joelle custody.'

A united front…not quite. Jude wouldn't be there. She hadn't seen or spoken to him in more than a week, and instead of coming to terms with losing him each day seemed bleaker than the one before. A cold front kept rolling through her soul.

She felt her throat clog with tears and swallowed them down. She'd cried enough but, despite telling herself she was done, more tears rose to the surface.

'Oh, Ads,' Lex murmured, wiping away Addi's tears with the tips of her fingers and pulling her into her arms. 'It'll get better, babe, I promise.'

The thing was, Addi thought as she sobbed into Lex's neck, she really didn't think it would.

Day nine, still no improvement. He still felt utterly miserable, completely shell-shocked.

Jude stood in his living room at his house in Franschhoek—he hadn't left his house since driving from Addi's house—and rested his forearm above his head, the glass cold beneath the fabric of his sweatshirt.

Night had rolled into the valley hours before and, by the light of the weak moon, he could see the outline of the jagged mountains just a few kilometres away. His heart felt equally jagged. It was almost as if it was struggling to pump blood around his body.

He'd thought he understood what heartbreak was, and had assumed he'd experienced all the lows a person could sink to. It was mortifying to realise he hadn't been even close to complete devastation.

He was now.

Back then, his heart had been dinged, but it had been his ego that had taken the biggest beating with Marina, and it had been smacked around again when Jane had sold him out. But he'd never once felt as though he was scrambling to find his feet in the seventeenth level of hell.

He missed Addi. No, saying that he simply missed her was like calling a nuclear missile a BB gun. This went beyond 'missing'…

Jude picked up his wine glass, sat on the edge of the leather couch and stared into his unlit fireplace. The truth was staring him in the face, demanding his attention, and he had to face it at some point. He couldn't possibly feel any worse than he did.

He'd messed up at various times, and with different results, but he'd kept blundering in, not thinking about what he was doing, saying or thinking, and hoping he'd emerge with nothing more than a slap on the wrist. That ended, right now.

He needed to up his game, and there was no option but for him to become a better man. A man worthy of someone as strong and special as Addi.

He rested his wine glass against his forehead. He'd had all the advantages of money and power, and had been spoiled rotten from the day he'd been born—yes, sure, he'd lost his parents, but he'd had the opportunity to attend an amazing school and get a stellar education. He'd had a ton of friends and girls had loved him. He'd led a very privileged life.

Sure, Marina had scammed him, but he'd been young and in love. Sure, she'd made a fool of him, but so what? And had she, *really*? Even at nineteen, he'd stuck by her, showing her far more loyalty than she'd deserved. He'd believed in her, believed what she told him. Surely he deserved praise for his loyalty?

And maybe it was time to put Marina, and that incident, in perspective. He'd been young, idealistic and she'd been older and skilled at the con. But nobody had died, and it had only been his and his grandfather's pride and ego—and a small portion of his heart—that had been hurt.

Instead of looking at the situation and brushing it off, he'd spent too many years nurturing the pain, giving it and his grandfather's mockery far more power than they deserved. He'd given that year of his life far too much importance, and too much mental energy. And, as a result, he'd started to believe that love was dangerous, that women couldn't be trusted.

Jane, and the humiliation of having his story appear in the papers, had reinforced that notion and scoured his soul even further, allowing cynicism and distrust to settle in, to flourish. Instead of responding to the newspaper articles with a laugh and shrugging his shoulders, telling the press that he'd been young and an idiot, his horrified and embarrassed response had made it a far juicier story than it had ever needed to be.

He, and old Bartholomew, had been the kings of the overreaction.

Marina had been a con artist, and Jane had been nasty, but that didn't follow that every woman was.

Addi certainly wasn't. She was a straight shooter, brave beyond belief, independent and feisty. She'd taken the knocks life had handed her without letting herself be knocked out. She'd simply stood up and kept fighting.

She was the bravest woman he knew.

From the moment she'd been small, she'd stepped up to the plate to look after her sister, to try and keep their ragtag family together. She'd worked her tail off to get her degree and, when she'd had the world at her feet, she'd sacrificed her freedom—financial and social—to take in her sisters.

Whether it was hard or not, Addi did what was right. She had more character and integrity than anyone he'd encountered before. She was the best person he knew…

And, for some reason, she loved him. And that was the biggest miracle of all.

She deserved far more from him than to keep their marriage secret and their affair under wraps. Far, far more. Miracles, love and second chances at happiness didn't come around all that often and he was pretty sure that he was running out of opportunities and second, or third, chances.

Maybe it was time he stopped moping and started *doing*.

This could backfire spectacularly, Jude thought as his driver dropped him off outside the courthouse where Addi and Lex were due to appear for the custody hearing. The girls, as Cole had told him, were in school and were being spared the ordeal of hearing a bunch of strangers argue about their future. Cole was accompanying Lex, but Addi would be by herself.

That wasn't, in any way, acceptable.

Dressed in a sharp grey suit, a white shirt and a patterned tie, Jude ran up the courthouse steps, imagining Addi sitting next to her lawyer, dressed in a severe suit, her show-no-fear mask on her face. He knew her—she would be quaking inside, but nobody would see her sweat.

Man, he hoped he made it into the courtroom on time…room seven, on the third floor, Judge Nkosi. He glanced at his watch and ran up the steps. The proceedings were about to start, and he didn't want to annoy the judge by walking in late. Jude found the right door, pulled it open and winced at its loud squeak. The room was silent, everyone was on their feet and they all turned to look at him.

Including Addi, her mouth dropping open in a perfect 'o'. He really hoped to kiss that mouth later. It had been too long since he'd held her, loved her. He needed to tell her that she was his, and vice versa, and that...

'Are you just going to stand there?'

The sharp voice intruded into his musings and Jude pulled his eyes off his wife to look at the judge. Her black hair was peppered with grey, bifocal glasses rested on her nose and her bright-red lipstick complemented her deep-brown skin.

Her eyes were sharper than a Katana sword.

'Who are you?' she demanded. 'And why are you late?'

Jude swallowed his grimace and out of the corner of his eye caught Cole's smirk. Jude used one hand to button his suit jacket as he approached the row of people standing behind the tables in front of the judge's dais. He looked to his left and caught a glimpse of Joelle, her long blonde hair hitting her waist. She looked like Addi's older sister.

'Again, who are you?'

Right. He really should start concentrating. Jude sent Addi a small smile and looked at the judge. 'My name is Jude Fisher—'

'Of Fisher International.'

'That's my company,' Jude confirmed. He loved it but it wasn't his life any more. He had a very different list of priorities now.

'And what relevance do you bring to this hearing, Mr Fisher?' Judge Nkosi asked, sounding impatient.

'Your Honour, I'm just here to support my *wife*,' Jude said as he stepped up to stand behind Addi, his hand on her waist.

'Mmm…' The judge grumbled and looked down. Feeling eyes on him, Jude looked down into Addi's lovely, upturned face—the face he wanted to spend the rest of his life looking into—and watched as shock skittered across it.

'I—what?' she snapped.

He shook his head, placed his hand on his back and bent down to whisper in her ear. 'Not now, sweetheart.'

As he straightened, Judge Nkosi looked up and lifted her eyebrows. 'Right, people, let's hear your arguments on who should get care of Miss Nixi and Miss Snow, and why. And please remember that the only side I am on is theirs…'

'My ruling is that the primary residence of the young ladies will be jointly shared by their eldest sisters. Their mother will be entitled to contact but, judging by her lack of interest in her youngest children,' Judge Nkosi stated, her disdain for Joelle clear, 'I doubt that she will use them. I am also ordering that Ms Cannon pay child maintenance of an amount to be decided, but I doubt that will happen either. Will it, Ms Cannon?'

'Probably not,' Joelle replied blithely.

Addi wondered why she wanted the girls back and then decided that she didn't much care. What Joelle did or didn't do had no bearing on her life any more. Her sisters and this baby were important, but her mother wasn't. Addi crossed her arms across her stomach, promising her baby that she'd be the amazing mother she'd never had. Loving, supporting and raising her child would be, for ever, her most important job.

Addi watched as Joelle dragged her eyes over Cole, then Jude. 'Sexy and rich. I taught you well,' she drawled. She raised an eyebrow at Storm. 'And what's your excuse?'

Addi heard Storm's growl and she grabbed the back of her shirt to keep her from confronting their mother. Luckily for all of them, Judge Nkosi banged her gavel and dismissed the court, suggesting that Joelle leave the premises ahead of her daughters.

Addi thought that was an excellent idea.

Feeling lightheaded, she sat down on the nearest hard-back chair, rested her arms on her thighs and dropped her head. She didn't know what to focus on first.

The girls were safe. Her family was intact. Jude was here.

He'd appeared when she'd most needed him and had stood behind her, his hand on her back, silently inviting her to lean on him.

From a place far, far away, she heard the sound of laughter, Storm's excited chatter and saw Lex hug Thandi. She heard Storm telling Jude to expect a lecture from Nixi and Snow because they'd missed out on the chance to be flower girls. Why wasn't Jude trying to hide their marriage any more? Instead of down-playing it, he'd announced it to everyone in the courtroom.

She heard Cole say something unintelligible and heard Thandi's equally indistinguishable reply.

The girls were safe. Her family was intact. Jude was here.

Addi felt a warm hand on her back and opened her eyes to see Jude on his haunches in front of her and then the world started to shrink. As she looked into his fantastic green eyes, she started to topple sideways...

And then...nothing.

Addi wrapped her head around a plush pillow and slowly opened her eyes. She was in her room at home and she could simply sleep for days.

She was about to slide back into sleep when she noticed there was sunlight on her bed. Sunlight meant that she'd taken a nap and she never took naps...ever.

Addi bolted upright, whipping her head round. The last thing she remembered was sitting down in the courthouse, feeling lightheaded because she and Lex had been granted custody of the girls.

Jude had been there. He'd confirmed the press reports that they were married.

Their secret was no longer a secret.

Addi pushed her fingers through her hair and looked down at the T-shirt she wore. It was one of Jude's. She'd taken to using it because it was soft and, no matter how many times it was washed, she could still smell his cologne on the fabric.

'Why are you sniffing that shirt?'

Lex looked up at Nixi's question and placed her hand on her chest as Nixi carefully, very carefully, carried a cup of tea into the room, followed by Snow carrying a plate of misshapen crumpets.

'We made you a snack,' Snow told her, thrusting the plate at her. Addi took the plate and kissed her bright-red head, doing the same to Nixi.

'Are you sick, Addi?' Nixi demanded, far too

seriously for an eight-year-old. She looked worried but stoic, and Addi realised she was in protective mode. This was how she would've looked at eight, she realised.

Addi gripped her chin in her hand and looked into her brown eyes. 'I'm not sick, baby girl, but if I was it's not your job to fix me. It's not your job to look after me, or Lex, or Storm, and it's definitely *not* your job to look after Snow. It's *our* job to look after you. Your job is to be a kid.'

'But—' Nixi said, looking mutinous.

Addi didn't give her a chance to speak. 'No buts, Nixi. We're the adults, you're the kid. Lex and I get to make the hard decisions, helped by Storm and—' she tossed a smile at Lex '—Cole. *We* look after *you*.'

'But who will look after you?' Snow asked, picking up on Nixi's anxiety.

'Well, that's *my* job.'

Addi looked past Lex and Storm, whose arms were around each other, tears rolling down their faces, to see Jude standing in the doorway to her bedroom, tie gone and sleeves rolled up. He brushed past her sisters and came to stand on the same side of the bed as Snow. He placed his hands on the bed and lowered his face so that it was inches from her own.

'Are you okay?' he asked.

She nodded, biting down on her bottom lip. 'I guess I was a little overwhelmed.'

A small smile kicked up the side of his mouth. 'I never thought anything could drop you to your knees, Fields.'

You do, she wanted to tell him.

Instead of throwing her arms around him as she desperately wanted to do, begging him to love her, she narrowed her eyes. 'Don't expect it to happen again, Fisher.'

'Who…are…you?'

They both turned to look at Nixi, her warrior princess looking as though she was about to defend her kingdom. Right; Addi would have to have a few more conversations about her role in their family. 'This is Jude and he is…'

She didn't know how to explain him. What was he? Legally, he was her husband, but he wasn't, not emotionally.

'I am the guy who is going to look after Addi so that she can look after you,' Jude told her, not moving an inch.

Nixi didn't look as if she was buying what he was selling. Addi, needing to know what he meant by that statement, leaned sideways and sent a pleading look at Lex and Storm who, bless them, immediately sprang into action. In what looked to be a choreographed move, they each wound an arm around a small waist, lifted the

girls off their feet and marched them to the door.
The door shut behind them and cut off their loud
and vociferous complaints.

Lex told them that if they didn't stop shouting
immediately they wouldn't be allowed to be her
flower girls, and silence descended.

Addi couldn't help but notice Jude didn't take
his eyes off her face.

'Hey,' he said, sitting down beside her.

She cocked her head and folded her arms
across her chest. 'I don't remember making my
way home.'

'You came to quite quickly after fainting, but
as soon as I picked you up to carry you to my
car you fell asleep. You've been sleeping for the
past five hours.'

Wow. 'That long?'

'I called your gynaecologist and she said that
it's probably a stress reaction. The body has a
way of shutting down eventually.'

'I guess it knew I could stop fighting and let
go,' Addi agreed.

She folded the material of the duvet between
her fingers and tried to work out how to ask him
why he'd announced to the courthouse, and her
family, that they were married. All it would do
was reignite the press's curiosity. 'Why did you
come to the courthouse and why did you…?'

'Tell everyone we were married?' He lifted

her hand and placed his mouth on her knuckles, his eyes on hers. 'Because wherever you are is where I should be. And because I want the world to know how lucky I am to call you my wife.'

'I don't understand, Jude.'

He dropped her hand, placed it on his thigh and held down her hand. 'I've made a couple of mistakes when it comes to trusting women, Ads, trusting people, but the mistakes weren't half as bad as I thought they were. Yes, I was conned by Marina, but I was a kid. I trusted Jane, I thought she had more integrity than she did. Yes, I failed, but we are allowed to fail, that's how we learn. But my stupidest, most thoughtless, asinine and dumb-ass decision was to lose you.'

He closed his eyes and gripped the bridge of his nose, looking as if he was in physical pain. 'These past ten days have been awful without you. I have missed you in every conceivable way. My comment in the airport was the biggest error I have ever made and one I've regretted every day, in every way, since. My only excuse is that I was scared.'

'Of?'

His eyes traced her face and, within them, she saw love, fear and, maybe, a little hope. 'Loving you, losing you, messing this up, taking a chance. From the moment I saw you at the Vane, you scrambled my brains. I'm still trying to work out which way is up.'

Jude leaned forward and placed his forehead against hers. 'I love you so much, Ads. I love the baby growing inside you but you, *you*, are my compass point. Nothing, *nothing*, is more important than you.'

Addi felt a fresh batch of tears roll down her face, but she felt lighter and brighter, as if her body was expelling the last of its angst and letting sunlight in. She lifted her arms to drape them around his neck. 'I love you too, Jude.' Her mouth drifted across his and, when their kiss deepened, she stepped into a band of pure, bright light, both calm and wonderfully exciting.

She was about to climb into his lap to get closer when Jude pulled back and the sound of childish giggles drifted over to her. Without missing a beat, she picked up a pillow and hurled it at the door with pinpoint accuracy. The door slammed shut again and they heard the sound of small feet scampering away.

'Sorry,' she whispered. 'They can be rather full-on.'

He grinned. 'I'll get used to it,' he told her. 'But we'll need to start locking the door.'

Jude moved to sit beside her on the bed and slung his arm around her, pulling her to his side.

This was where she belonged, she thought. Right here. Wherever he was.

'What now?' she asked, resting her hand on his flat stomach.

He placed a kiss on her head. 'Well, you have a few options. After talking to Cole, it looks like Storm is going to use the apartment above the garage on his mini-estate and he's employing an au pair for the girls so Lex can finish her degree. You can move into his cottage, stay here or...'

None of those options appealed. 'Or...?'

'Or we live together here, or at my flat, and spend the weekends with or without the girls at my place in Franschhoek. Or we can go house-shopping and try and find something new, close to Cole and Lex's house, a place big enough for the girls to stay over when Lex and Cole need a break.'

She was about to tell him that she was keen on that option when he held up his hand. 'I need to say something else...'

She pulled back, a little concerned, and waited anxiously while he found his words. 'I know how independent you are, and I know I promised you a job at Fisher—and it's there, any time you want it.'

'But?'

'But I'd like you to take a break. I'd like you to let me take care of you. You've had the incredible responsibility of making all the decisions all the time, the stress of making money stretch and keeping this family together, and I would like you to take a few months off. I can't see you not working—you need the stimulation. I'm thinking that maybe, when you are ready to jump back in, you could act as a trouble-shooter for Fisher, or maybe manage your own group of hotels.'

Huh. 'I don't have a group of hotels, Jude.'

He mock-grimaced. 'Well, you kind of do. I've signed all of my eco-hotels and lodges, the ones I bought in my personal capacity, over to you. Oh, and I also bought the boutique hotel on the Skeleton Coast for you, but I suspect we'll keep that as our bolthole.'

She now owned the Dune House? And she had a small hotel chain? 'You…? What…? But *why*?'

'Call it a wedding gift. Call it a thank you for my baby, my gratitude for you loving me. It's also a promise that, whatever we do and wherever we go, we do it together. Deal?'

Her head was spinning. 'Um…you could've just bought me a ring, Fisher,' she said, sounding breathless.

He leaned to the side and pulled a box out of his trouser pocket. He flipped it open with his thumb and Addi gulped at the magnificent ring comprising three huge stones—an emerald, a deep-blue sapphire and what she thought was a pink diamond. 'I figured we're going to have a girl,' he told her, laughing.

Yep, probably. He slid it onto the ring finger of her left hand and lifted her hand to his lips. 'So, shall we get married, Ads?'

'We *are* married,' she told him, laughing.

'Let's do it properly this time…'

* * * * *

If you were blown away by
The Baby Behind Their Marriage Merger
then make sure to check out the first instalment of the Cape Town Tycoons duet
The Nights She Spent with the CEO

And why not dive into these other captivating stories by Joss Wood?

How to Tempt the Off-Limits Billionaire
The Rules of Their Red-Hot Reunion
The Billionaire's One-Night Baby
The Powerful Boss She Craves
The Twin Secret She Must Reveal

Available now!